T

Colusa County Free Library

738 Market Street
Colusa, CA   95932
Phone : 458-7671

Return
of the Spanish

Return
of the Spanish

》》 》》 》》 》》 》》 》》 》》 》》 》》 》》 》》 》》 》》

DON COLDSMITH

A Double D Western
Doubleday
NEW YORK   LONDON   TORONTO   SYDNEY   AUCKLAND

A DOUBLE D WESTERN
PUBLISHED BY DOUBLEDAY
a division of Bantam Doubleday Dell Publishing Group, Inc.
666 Fifth Avenue, New York, New York 10103

DOUBLE D WESTERN, DOUBLEDAY,
and the portrayal of the letters DD
are trademarks of Doubleday, a division of
Bantam Doubleday Dell Publishing Group, Inc.

Library of Congress Cataloging-in-Publication Data

Coldsmith, Don, 1926–
Return of the Spanish / Don Coldsmith.—1st ed.
    p.   cm.—(A Double D western)
"The Spanish bit saga book 18."
    1. Indians of North America—Great Plains—Fiction. I. Title.
PS3553.O445R39   1991
813'.54—dc20   90-23387
CIP

14.95

ISBN 0-385-26302-3
Copyright © 1991 by Don Coldsmith
All Rights Reserved
Printed in the United States of America
May 1991
First Edition

91 B5236

10   9   8   7   6   5   4   3   2   1

Time Period: 1720

Return
of the Spanish

Prologue
›› ›› ››

The Governor sat at his desk and reread the letter for the third time. His fingers toyed with the parchment, and with the fragments of broken wax seal. It was the official seal of the government in Mexico City, seat of the Spanish overseas empire, New Spain.

He seldom heard from Mexico City. The upper echelons of government had long ignored the province of New Mexico. It had been nearly thirty years now since Spain had returned to the provincial capital at Santa Fe. Diego de Vargas had restored the Spanish claim to the province, after a twelve-year absence resulting from the pueblo rebellion. Governor Valverde remembered having heard about that war as a child. That must have been a bloody summer. The natives had risen up to overthrow their Spanish rulers, killing large numbers, and driving the survivors south, all the way to El Paso del Norte, the gateway back into Mexico. Little had he imagined that someday he would be appointed Governor of that reclaimed province. But it had happened. Apparently the entire rebellion had been organized and held together by one man, a native medicine man from Taos. According to some, this man had proved a tyrant to his own people, and his death a few years later was little mourned.

That had made it possible for Vargas to recover the province for the Crown with virtually no bloodshed. The situation had been calm ever since. Valverde, when the appointment as Governor had come to him, was not certain what to expect. He had found it quite pleasant. The climate was comfortable, much preferable to any of the cities where he had served before. The natives were moderately quiet and content, since being re-Christianized by Vargas' friars. All in all, it was a comfortable assignment, far enough from the political intrigue at home to avoid most problems. As long as he kept a low profile, those above him in the chain of command bothered him very little. He administered the province largely from his office desk in the old Palace of Governors, and enjoyed the prestige due to one in his position. Yes, life was good.

He tilted back his chair and stared out the window, across the promenade and the plaza beyond. Why did this letter have to intrude just now? Well, at *any* time, actually. It would have been so much easier to ignore the problems of the world, to sit here in his own little domain, a quiet back-eddy of the mainstream of commerce.

But this letter . . . a direct order, not to be ignored. A military expedition . . . *Mother of God,* he thought, *how uncomfortable.* He would be sleeping on the ground again, doing without the creature comforts that had become so much a part of his life as Governor of New Mexico. This was 1720, not the primitive days of exploration and colonization. Why had the cursed French wanted to thrust into the continent, anyway?

Such changes happened so quickly. There had sometimes been contact and trade with French outposts a few
years ago. Contact that had actually been rather pleasant, a touch of sophistication on the bleak frontier. But
no longer. Now, their countries were at war in Europe,
and this lent a whole different light. Ah, well . . .

His thoughts were interrupted by the sight of a figure
strolling across the plaza. *Villasur,* he thought. Of
course! A perfect answer to his dilemma. He had wanted
a way for young Villasur to acquire a bit more experience in command, and here it was, made to order. Even
as he finished the thought, Governor Valverde leaned
forward to call to his orderly in the outer office.

"Gomez! Please ask the Lieutenant Governor to join
me!"

"Yes, señor."

"He is in the plaza now."

"Yes."

The orderly's boots made a quick tattoo on the plank
floor as he hurried down the corridor and into the spring
sunshine. In only a few moments the Governor heard
the echo of returning footsteps.

Pedro de Villasur paused at the door of the Governor's
office and then stepped inside.

"You wished to see me, Excellency?"

Valverde studied the newcomer for a moment. Villasur was a fine figure of a man, young and ambitious. His
present position, as vice-governor, gave the young man
little opportunity. Valverde suspected that the position
must be boring to his lieutenant. Now, however, this
turn of events might provide an excellent opportunity.
Villasur could be relieved of the boredom of his somewhat superfluous office. At the same time, he would have
the experience of a military command, in the field. It was
a situation that the Governor suspected hardly war-
ranted a campaign. He really doubted that the French

were a major threat to New Mexico. But no matter. He motioned his visitor to a chair.

"Sit down, Villasur."

He rose, walked over to close the door, and returned to the chair behind his desk.

"Is there a problem, Governor?"

"What? No, no. Only a situation with which I need your help."

He watched the younger man broaden with pleasure, and allowed him to bask in it for a moment. Then he continued.

"I have here a letter from Mexico City," he stated, waving the parchment dramatically. Valverde had not risen to his present position without knowing how to exploit the drama in a situation.

"As you know," he went on, "the French are claiming the territory along the Great River . . . the Missiseppe."

He paused to unroll a map on his desk, and held it in place with an inkwell and a container of blotting sand, at opposite edges.

"Here," he continued. "Here is Santa Fe . . . here, the trail from the northeast. There are French forts there, at the junction of two great rivers."

"I see," Villasur agreed. "How far, señor?"

"That is uncertain. Two, maybe three months' journey. The natives are quite vague about distance, you know."

Villasur nodded. "But what . . . ?"

"I am coming to that," said the Governor impatiently. "Now, there have been rumors of attacks in Tejas . . . here . . ." He pointed. "Natives armed and led by French officers."

The eyes of the Lieutenant Governor widened in wonder.

"Now, I doubt this," Valverde continued. "However, I

have received orders . . . this letter. We are to send an expedition . . ."

"To *Tejas?*" Villasur interrupted.

"No, no. Toward the area of their forts . . . here, in the country of the Kenzas." He pointed to the map again. "I want you to lead such an expedition . . . *northeast.*"

Pedro de Villasur's mouth sagged open with astonishment.

"*Me,* señor?"

"Of course. It will be good experience, a taste of command. You will take forty soldiers, and a like number of our Christian natives. A priest . . . and we have found a French renegade who will act as interpreter if needed. You can enlist the locals as guides as you travel."

Villasur's thoughts had come to a stop some time back in the Governor's explanation.

"Forty men?" he asked. "Half the garrison?"

"Yes. If you encounter the French, let it be with a show of force. Now, here is your route. Oh, yes, one other thing . . . We have heard rumors of natives who left the province at the time of the war. Some have built towns on the plains, east of the mountains. I want you to find any of these strays that you can, and entice them back to New Mexico. Your priest can rebaptize, and assure them that all is forgiven."

"If I may ask, Excellency," Villasur said cautiously, "*why?*"

"Because they are skilled farmers. Our province is not as productive as it was before the war. You have seen the abandoned pueblos. If we can make a good showing, an increase in crops and goods, we will look prosperous to the authorities. Then they will let us alone, to follow our course."

To appear prosperous and stable, but not excitingly so, Valverde had decided. It had bothered him to see the idle plots that he knew had once produced crops. Villasur's mission might as well be a twofold one.

"When will this expedition take place?" asked the still surprised Villasur.

"Soon . . . hmm . . . that is a long journey, and it is nearly June. Yes, to be back before winter, you should start as soon as possible. When could you be ready?"

The Governor was thinking even as he spoke. A day or two to assemble supplies, ready the troops. Possibly a day longer to organize the natives who would go. They never seemed to understand the urgency of anything. But he would let Villasur make the decision for the departure. That was one of the primary purposes of the mission, after all. It would allow the growth and maturation of the Lieutenant Governor's administrative skills. Valverde was pleased, therefore, when Villasur answered quickly and confidently.

"I would think, Excellency, that I might start within the week."

1

>> >> >>

South Wind sat with her husband and watched the young men at their contest. She was very proud of Strong Bow, their youngest son.

He was the child of their old age. She had thought, in fact, that she was past the age of childbearing. Her older son, Red Horse, was grown and about to be married, when her menstrual cycles had ceased. It was some concern that her belly had begun to swell, but not until she felt the movement within her did she suspect the truth, that another child was to join their lodge.

It was good, of course. The infant was easygoing and cheerful, and a comfort to her in the emptiness of a lodge that was no longer made busy by the comings and goings of young people. Strong Bow, he was called. At first it was because of the well-muscled arms, and a remark by Red Feather, the child's proud grandfather, that he would someday draw a powerful weapon. But the name seemed to fit, and the growing boy wore it with pride.

He took interest in the use of the bow, and practiced with it incessantly.

As he grew stronger, so did the succession of weapons whose name he bore. His skill became a matter of pride for his parents. Strong Bow was only a little older than the children of his brother, Red Horse.

Aiee, thought South Wind now, how much had happened to her family! She and White Fox had met during his vision-quest at Medicine Rock, how long ago, now? Nearly forty summers! They had been fortunate, there, to escape with their lives. There had been exciting times, too, for their son, Red Horse. There was much pride in his accomplishments. He had restored the white buffalo cape to the People; powerful medicine!

But for this one, Strong Bow, life had been rather uneventful. He had not yet been born when the family accompanied the French exploring party on the river . . . a disastrous expedition! The People had experienced good times and bad since that time, but none of it had affected this one of her children. The threats which had faced them had somehow passed him by, because of his age and status at each crisis. Strong Bow remained a happy, well-liked youth, enjoying the strength of his young manhood.

And Strong Bow, though fully grown now, nearly twenty winters of age, still lived in the lodge of his parents. Though he was one of the most eligible bachelors of the People, he had not yet married. Some wondered if perhaps his sexual preference pointed in other directions, but it was not so. He appreciated the attraction of feminine curves, of long, well-formed legs, and beauty of face and figure. He had had many friends among the girls in the Rabbit Society as they grew up together and participated in the learning process of the young.

He had admired strength and capability in a woman. Perhaps he had inherited that from his parents. He had heard the story of how his mother had survived alone at the Rock before she and his father had first met. There had been many capable women among those his own age, and these were his friends, as were the boys with whom he competed. But they had been only that . . . friends. No real romance had developed, and one by one, his friends had married and set up their own lodges. The attitude of Strong Bow toward this was much like that toward all of life, good-natured and easy. What would happen would happen in due time, whenever the time was appropriate.

So he had grown up. One has small children only a little while, South Wind reflected, a little sadly. She saw his present status, single and living at home, with mixed feelings. She would have been pleased to see him in his own lodge, with a good wife and children of his own. On the other hand, she had grandchildren already, and it was good to have her son, the baby of her later years, come home to her lodge and greet his mother with a warm embrace.

Yet, despite all of this, she felt restless and unfulfilled, somehow. She did not know exactly what it was. It would soon be time for the Sun Dance, and they would meet the other bands. That would be an interesting and exciting time.

It was a prosperous year for the People. They had survived the years of drought, and their medicine was strong. The children were fat and the women happy. There had been a return to the security of the old ways, at least in spirit. There were a few modern innovations. Some used flint and steel to start their fires, instead of the fire-sticks, but few saw this as offensive to the old spirits. Times were good.

Why, then, did she feel this restlessness? There seemed to be something unfulfilled, a longing of some sort. Maybe it was only the odd call of the spirit that one feels each spring when the geese fly north, the longing to follow their trail. Surely, there is something of a thrill to watch the long lines of great birds honking their way across the clear blue of the heavens. There is the curiosity, the wonder at the sights they will see, and the wish to share their experiences. But she felt that every year in the Moon of Awakening. This was something else.

Her husband was looking at her as if he expected her to speak. She realized that he must have spoken to her, and was awaiting an answer.

"What? . . . I am sorry . . . I was thinking." She pulled herself back to reality. "What did you say?"

White Fox was laughing at her now.

"You were far away," he chided. "Where were you? Back in the cave at Medicine Rock?"

"No, I . . ." she began, but then stopped.

Maybe that was it. She had adapted quite well to this nomadic life with her husband's people, but it was far different from that of her childhood. And, strange as that had been, alone with her half-demented grandfather, it had provided a sense of *place*. She had felt a similar sense of belonging when they had visited the pueblo village of her husband's grandparents. At this time of year, Moon Flower's people would be preparing to plant. Corn, beans, pumpkins. They would come out of the pueblos and go to the fields, with the appropriate songs and prayers of the Elders, and carefully nestle the seeds into the warm, mealy earth. Even now she could remember, the closeness to the earth that she had felt, the feel in her fingers, the loamy smell . . .

"Maybe we should visit your mother's people," she suggested. "We have not been there for several summers."

Several summers. Yes, it was true. The grandparents of White Fox were dead now, of course, but there were other relatives. Uncles, cousins, nephews and nieces.

Moon Flower's father had been the leader of a pueblo that had elected not to participate in the war forty summers ago. People from several of these villages had left their traditional homeland and traveled northeast, away from the familiar mountains and sandy desert, out onto the plains to resettle. This group had built a pueblo in a canyon on the plain, in the range of the People, and planted their crops in unfamiliar terrain. They had been successful here, being normally peaceful and tolerant by nature. They had traded with the hunter-nations for meat and robes.

Red Feather and Moon Flower had considered it important to visit her people, and for their children to learn of this part of their heritage. White Fox had continued the tradition. Their visits were less frequent, now. The drought years had come, and there was more attention to survival than to social amenities. Then, it was not quite so easy to travel now, as aging bones voiced their complaints on chilly mornings. Yes, it was several years since they had even considered such a trip. And Strong Bow had been there only a time or two. Maybe it was time.

"Could we?" Wind asked. "It would be good for Strong Bow to meet his cousins again now that they are grown. I would like that."

Her husband smiled.

"You always liked to visit there. Well, why not? After the Sun Dance, when the bands move on for the summer, we will go there."

"It is good!"

She clapped her hands in delight, like a child, and White Fox smiled. That was one of her mannerisms that he loved.

"Good. The Sun Dance is at Sandy River, so it will not be a difficult journey. Maybe Red Horse will bring his family and go with us."

"I think not, Fox. He is very busy as holy man, now. The white cape . . ."

"That is true. Maybe not. But we will tell Strong Bow tonight."

2
>> >> >>

Strong Bow was enthusiastic, of course, in his own quiet way. He had always been so, adjusting easily to any change in plans. His was the easygoing approach of the People . . . one day at a time, to each its own problems. But why worry about tomorrow, until one knows what problems it will present?

They talked of the journey, and invited Red Horse and his family to join them in this reunion. After some consideration, Horse and his wife, Swallow, agreed. It would be good for their children, to meet relatives in the pueblo.

With the decision behind them, it was now merely waiting, undertaking daily tasks, and looking forward to the coming of the Moon of Roses. That would bring the Sun Dance, and in turn the journey to the pueblo. South Wind found that, now she had the coming visit to anticipate, her restlessness had subsided. She could look forward with pleasure not only to the reunion but to the journey itself. It should be a pleasant time, the prairie green and lush and dotted with flowers. The Moon of Roses was well named. She loved the variety of colors that the roses displayed, from almost white to deep smoky reds. And their scent . . . Ah, it was a good time to be alive. There were other flowers, too, the snowy white of daisies with yellow centers, the brilliant fiery orange of the butterfly-flowers.

But first, the Sun Dance. That in itself was the biggest event of the year, a combination of religious ceremony, games and contests, family reunions, and visits with friends not seen since last season. All of the five bands of the nation would meet at a predetermined place, to camp together for as long as nearly a moon. The official ceremonies lasted seven days and nights, after days of preparation. Dancers would drop out, to be replaced by others, day in and day out, with the drums and songs never ceasing.

There was also the Big Council, usually on the evening after the arrival of the last band. That was usually the Eastern band, whose ineptness was a traditional joke among the People. In addition, there was a short cere-monial wait for a now extinct band whose name had been all but forgotten. There was an empty place in the circle of the Council, reserved for the Other band. It was known that they would never return, but the space was kept open in their memory. They had left the People, and had been exterminated by their enemies, it was said, before the nation moved southward many generations ago.

South Wind had always been fascinated by all this in-teraction among people. Her lonely upbringing, know-ing no one except her grandfather, had not prepared her for this. She had not missed it, of course, because she had no way to know that it existed. The excitement of her first Sun Dance had been almost overwhelming. She was a little bit afraid. There were so many people. But White

Fox and his family had been extremely supportive. Now, after so many seasons, there was only the excitement and anticipation, the joy of celebration of the return of the sun, the grass, and the buffalo.

She loved to watch the young men as they celebrated the strength of their young manhood. As each band joined the encampment, those already there would leap on their horses and perform a mock charge at the new-comers. The combined group would then sweep to-gether in a mighty circle around the camp. The thunder of the hundreds of pounding hooves was enough to set one's heart to pounding, and the blood coursing through the head. Sometimes the race came too close to the outer lodges, and women would come out to yell irritably at the revelers about the dust that drifted into the camp.

"You may like dirt in your food, stupid ones," one woman shouted, "but we do not! Go away!"

But mostly, the spirit of the occasion was exciting enough to overcome the annoyance of being together in a large camp. Besides, it was only for a short time. It was well worth any slight inconvenience.

The weather held, fine sunny days and cool nights, the sky of the brightest blue. Truly, there was no time of the year like the Moon of Roses.

During the festival of the Sun Dance, South Wind and White Fox prepared for the coming journey. There were supplies to assemble, garments and spare moccasins, the selection of horses. Arrangements were made for rela-tives to transport their lodge and store it. The summer camp of the Southern band would be at Broken-Arm Creek.

"We will join you there, before the move to winter camp," South Wind assured Deer Woman. "Maybe we will not even set up the lodge until the band moves."

"It is good," replied Deer Woman. "Do not worry. We

will take care of everything. May you have a good summer!"

Strong Bow, between participation in the ceremonial dances, contests, and races, chose their horses. A sturdy, gentle mare for his mother, a rugged gelding with smooth gaits for White Fox. For himself, two animals. One was his favorite buffalo runner, a strong stallion with an approach from the right of a running animal. This favored the use of the bow, his namesake and weapon of choice. This horse was not used for anything but the chase, so another was needed for transportation, a sturdy dun with good muscle and flint-hard hooves. Two pack horses to carry their supplies completed the little caravan. Red Horse and his family would provide their own horses. The rest of the horses belonging to both families would be herded with those of the entire Southern band until fall, when they rejoined the group.

At the end of the Sun Dance, when the big lodges began to come down, one of the first of them was the lodge of South Wind and Fox. If one has a journey, it is necessary to start. By the time the Mountain band was ready to go, South Wind was growing impatient. They would travel with this band for much of the way, since they were going in the same direction. There should be no danger. The People had no enemies at this time. They had had none for a couple of generations. The plains were quiet. Still, it was a reassuring thing to travel with a larger group. One could never tell. And the band would have scouts or "wolves" circling the caravan, as the big gray wolves circle a buffalo herd for a more sinister purpose. The wolves of the People would warn of any danger, any strangers approaching.

They camped the first night far to the northwest of the Sun Dance site. It was a beautiful place, the prairie green with the lush growth of early summer. White Fox and South Wind walked to a slight rise to enjoy the sunset.

From this spot, a bow shot or two above the camp, they could look across the prairie in any direction, to the rim of the earth, it seemed. The gray-green of the short buffalo grass contrasted with the richer greens of the taller prairie grasses in the gullies and watershed areas. Willows and cottonwoods along the stream provided even darker green color. This winding stripe narrowed to blend into a sameness of bluish hues that distance created. It was flatter, more level country than the Sacred Hills of home, but pleasant. A south breeze cooled the evening.

Along the stream below, people were starting campfires. They were not needed for warmth, or actually for cooking. It was more of a ritual, a declaration of being . . . *here we intend to be, tonight.* There was a sense of communication with whatever spirits might dwell here. An apology for intrusion, perhaps, yet a statement of good will and of a right to be here, all at once. Strong Bow would be helping with the fire of Red Horse and Swallow, which would serve both families.

No one would set up the big skin lodges tonight. It was not worth the trouble, for one sleep. The weather was good, anyway. Some would make flimsy brush shelters from willows along the creek, but mostly they would sleep under the stars. South Wind smiled contentedly as she listened to the faint hum of human activity from below. It was good, the buzz of conversation, the occasional shout of a child at play, the soft noises from the direction of the horse herd, held together in a little meadow downstream. A horse nickered, searching for a companion from which it had become separated, and the other answered.

She turned to watch the changing colors of the western sky. Sun Boy's torch was nearing earth's rim, and the flaming colors were splashed across the entire west, as he painted himself for the crossing to his lodge on the other side.

"Sun Boy chooses his paints well tonight," Wind observed.

"Yes."

What more could be said? The pink of the scattered summer clouds was giving way to a glorious celebration of reds, golden yellows, and blues, changing before their eyes to deeper, richer hues. Now the darker colors were deepening to purple, as shadows lengthened across the prairie. They crept up, out of low places and stream beds, growing and stretching, blending together and spreading. Then the last bright rays of Sun Boy's torch slipped beyond the rim and the shadows vanished. The prairie was now covered by the soft robe of twilight, uniform in its blue-gray consistency. The sky still held a glow in the west, lighting the world for a little longer with an otherworldly warmth.

Even that light was fading fast. A bright point of light appeared in the west, as the first star of the evening made its appearance. White Fox pointed, without speaking. Wind nodded.

"Yes," she said simply.

They watched a little while longer, as more stars appeared, one by one. The creatures of the night were coming awake, with their distinctive noises, as those of the day sought their lodges for rest. From somewhere downstream came the hollow call of a hunting owl.

"*Kookooskoos!*" chuckled Red Horse. "His people are everywhere!"

The call sounded again, from another direction, and soon a shadowy form flitted noiselessly past, low against the darkening sky.

"Good hunting, *Kookooskoos,*" Horse called softly.

A distant coyote chortled. It could have been in any direction, because coyote can throw his voice quite cleverly, but Horse pointed to a low hilltop to the south. Yes, there was motion there. A pair of coyotes, most likely, teaching their pups to hunt.

"Let us go down," said Red Horse. "Our pups will wonder what has happened to us."

South Wind chuckled, and they turned toward the camp, hand in hand.

3

>> >> >>

Strong Bow hardly remembered their last visit to the pueblo. He had been much younger, no more than ten summers old. Even so, he began to recall things about that summer as they approached the general area where his grandmother's people had made their home after the war with the Spanish.

They had traveled across country that was increasingly dry and treeless for several days. The creatures of this drier country were different, as were the plants and grasses. There was stark contrast with the lush summer growth of the Tallgrass Hills, where the Southern band loved to make their summer camps.

They passed large towns of the ground-burrowing creatures that reminded him of a large squirrel with no tail. It was virtually impossible to get a close look at one of them, because at the mere approach of any larger animal, they would give a sharp, whistling bark of warning and dive into their lodges. Then there would be only the hundreds of low mounds on the flat plain. Each mound appeared to be formed of the sand and earth which had been removed in the process of digging the underground burrow.

It was amusing to watch the creatures. When they emerged again from their lodges, they would sit bolt upright, each stiffly posed on the top of its mound. The forelegs were held tightly against the chest, as the animal sat up on its haunches to stretch and see farther across the plain. Its appearance was that of a short, stout stick or peg in the ground, like the stakes used to peg down the edges of a lodge skin.

They moved on, generally westward now, following the course of the river upstream. The stream grew smaller in this drier country, now. The creeks that joined it were smaller, too. Sometimes the mouth of a tributary was completely dry, marked only by the cutbank in the sandy soil.

Strong Bow wondered how his relatives could grow their crops in an area which received such sparse rainfall. He really had no knowledge, or interest, in such things as growing crops. It was useful to have Growers at hand, with whom to trade. There were usually extra meat and robes to trade, after the fall hunts, for corn and beans and pumpkins. And these were good, in the long moons of winter, to vary the sameness of dried meat and pemmican. Still, to Strong Bow, the ways of the People seemed preferable. He could not imagine living in one of the permanent lodges of the Growers on the prairie streams in their familiar Tallgrass country.

He had been in one of their lodges, once. When he was a small child, the Southern band had camped near a Grower village for a few days of trading. He had been playing with Grower children. He could speak none of their tongue, but this is no barrier to the young. There is a universal understanding between children at play, those of any tribe or nation. For some reason, this is lost to adults.

In this case, he had accompanied a boy about his own age to the other's lodge. It was a strange structure, made of logs and sticks, dug partly into the ground and heaped over with dirt. Curiously, he had followed his friend down into the dusky cave.

He was well inside before the fear struck him. Perhaps it had been the smell . . . a close, musty animal smell, the odor of human beings in close quarters. Suddenly, Strong Bow had felt trapped, enclosed. He fled, turning to rush into the open, to fill his lungs with fresh air, where one could breathe freely again. His friend had followed him with concern, but there was no way to explain. If one does not feel such a threat, there is no way to tell him of it.

From that time on, Strong Bow had avoided such dwellings. He had no animosity toward Growers, and in fact respected their useful pursuits. It was simply that he did not wish to live in a hole in the ground. It was good for those who wished to do so. The eagle builds his lodge in the tree, the quail and grouse on the grassy sod, and the fox in the soil, and this is as it should be. But it was not for a hunter who rides a horse, with the wind rushing past his body and his hair streaming back from the speed of the chase . . . *Aiee,* how could a man spend his days hoeing corn?

This was the feeling of the young man on this day as they rode upriver. He was interested in the ways of others, but not for himself. Only as an observer. He knew, of course, that his relatives did not live in earth-lodges like that which had frightened him as a child. He remembered the pueblo, the strange, square lodges made of sunbaked mud bricks. At least, they were above the ground. Anyway, the visitors would not have to stay inside. The weather would probably permit sleeping under the stars. They could take temporary shelter in case of rain.

But one question continued to gnaw at him. The country they were traversing now was quite dry, and becoming more so. It was not that it was a dry season. It was apparent that in this area, *every* season was dry. At least, drier than the Tallgrass Hills. And, little as he knew about the ways of Growers, he knew that for plants to grow there must be water.

He sought out his older brother.

"Horse," he asked as they rode ahead of the party for a little while, "how is it that they can grow corn in such a place?"

"What do you mean?"

"It is dry here, and becoming more so."

"Did you want to grow corn, little brother?" Red Horse teased.

Strong Bow's love for the hunt was well known.

"No, be serious, Horse! I only wondered. If one is a grower, would he not look for the best places?"

Red Horse laughed, but his laugh was no longer one of teasing. His wisdom as a holy man was well respected among the People, though he was still young. He had seen much.

"It is as you say, brother. But each does as he must. Fish swim, birds fly, rabbits run. And the people of the pueblos, the family of our grandmother, grow corn. Our father says that they come from a much drier place than this."

"*Aiee!* Drier yet?"

"Yes, so he says. It was their place, as the Tallgrass Hills are our place, our Sacred Hills. They left there only because of the war."

"But the corn . . ."

"Yes. They have grown corn in dry places for many

generations. That is their way, as fish swim, and snakes crawl."

"But *how?*"

"It is a thing of the spirit, maybe. They plant carefully, and carry water to thirsty plants, but mostly, I think, it is their medicine. You or I could not grow corn, as they do."

"*Aiee!* I would not want to!"

Red Horse laughed.

"Of course. That is plain. You would rather chase buffalo."

Strong Bow laughed, too.

"That is true. But is this a special corn?"

"Yes. That is partly it. They have a corn that is blue. Did you know that our ancestor, the Elder who brought them here, was named that? Blue Corn?"

"I had forgotten . . . he was the father of Moon Flower?"

"Yes, that is the one. He led his people away from the war. But the blue corn . . . it is part of their medicine."

"Ah, I see. It needs little water?"

"Partly that, but more. Its spirit, that of the corn, is one with theirs. There are songs, prayers, to make the corn grow. For rain, too."

"I have heard of that. Can their holy men really make it rain, Horse?"

"Maybe," Red Horse said equivocally.

"Can your medicine do it?"

Red Horse was quiet a moment, lost in thought. When he did speak, it was quietly, and very seriously.

"Strong Bow," he began, "the medicine of the People is different. Mine is of the buffalo and the grass, the horse and hunting on the prairie. This is our life. It falls to me to wear the bit, the elk-dog medicine, which helps us control the horse."

"Yes, I know of this. The white cape, too."

Strong Bow could remember the marvelous amulet,

the Spanish horse bit with its silver dangles, hanging in
the place of honor in their father's lodge. White Fox had
worn it on a thong around his neck for special ceremoni-
als, such as the Sun Dance, or to pray for success in the
hunt. The holy man had handed the bit down to his son
Red Horse after Horse had restored the white buffalo
cape to the tribe a few seasons ago. Strong Bow remembered that excitement well, though he was but a child at
the time.

"But, Horse . . ." he began.

His brother waved him to silence.

"Do you remember," Horse asked, "when I returned
with the white cape?"

"Of course. But what . . ."

Horse seemed lost in thought.

"I saw many things," he recalled. "There was a holy
man that I met."

"Of the pueblo people?"

"No, of another nation. I do not know. But his medicine was powerful. He danced for rain."

Now Strong Bow was confused.

"What has this to do with anything, Horse?"

Red Horse smiled.

"Nothing. Except his medicine was different from
mine. Each nation's, even each holy man's medicine, is
different. Now, you have asked about the rainmaking of
the people we go to visit. What you wish to know is how
they do it."

Strong Bow felt embarrassed, and a little ashamed. He
knew now what his brother was trying to say. One does
not ask about another's medicine, as such a gift is a very
private thing. To question it would be quite impolite at
best.

"Yes," Strong Bow admitted. "Forgive me, Horse. I
would not ask of your medicine."

His brother nodded.

"True. And we should not ask of theirs."

They rode in silence a little way, and finally Red Horse chuckled.

"But it would be interesting to know. Come, I will race you to that tree!"

Although middle-aged, and the most respected holy man among the People, there were times when Red Horse seemed an impetuous youth. Strong Bow was caught off guard as his brother kicked heels into his horse's flanks and shot forward like an arrow from the bowstring. Bow hammered his own horse's sides. His mount flattened his ears and stretched like a great cat, long strides striving to overtake the other animal.

It was a foolish, boyish thing to do, racing during a journey on the trail. A horse could easily be injured, running at top speed on unfamiliar terrain. One stumble, a foot in one of the lodge-holes of the tailless squirrels . . . a good horse could be destroyed in the space of a heartbeat. But that was easy to ignore, in the thrill of the pounding hooves and the rush of the wind.

The tree that marked the race's finish was several hundred paces away. Strong Bow's horse was gaining on the other, but not enough. It was apparent that Red Horse would reach the lone cottonwood first. Strong Bow relaxed, laughing at the boyishness of his older brother. Their father would probably reprimand them both, if he had chanced to see the race.

Ahead of him, Horse had reached the tree and pulled his mount to a stop. Strong Bow joined him, but Red Horse was looking on, far to the west.

"Look," he said, pointing.

In the distance, a wandering line of trees indicated a sizable stream bed, which joined the one on which they traveled. Its course must be from the south, then. Most of the streams, Strong Bow recalled, had entered from the north. There was something different here.

"What is it?" he asked.

Red Horse chuckled.

"You do not remember . . . you were small."

"Remember what?"

"The stream . . . it flows *north* into the river. The only one in the area which flows in that direction. That is the one where our pueblo relatives live. We have arrived!"

He turned his horse and started back, but at a walk. Both animals were blowing hard after their hard run.

"We must tell the others!" called Red Horse.

It would have been tempting to ride on ahead, but Strong Bow drew his horse into line beside his brother's mount. There was custom and protocol to observe, and it should be that for a family visit they arrived as a family, out of respect for their parents.

4

>> >> >>

It was still most of an afternoon's ride to the pueblo village. They soon saw evidence of human activity. A thin haze of cooking smoke hung over the narrow ribbon of trees in the distance. There were signs of habitation . . . a general scarcity of any dead wood in trees and bushes along the streams and gullies. Any such sticks had long since been used as fuel for cooking and for warmth against the harsh prairie winters. There were also paths through the sparse buffalo grass, and in the more lush growth nearer the streams. Their meandering patterns suggested that these paths were once animal trails. Quite likely they still were, worn not only by generations of deer, fox, and coyote, but also by generations of moccasined feet.

They approached the tributary, and veered to the south to follow its course. It was still some time before they could see patches of growing corn below the rim of the shallow canyon that they were now following. A youth who had been tending crops stood staring at the

approaching party for a moment and then darted away
to spread the news of visitors. In only a moment he had
disappeared among the fluttering leaves of the corn.

The newcomers proceeded at their leisurely pace, and
soon sighted the expected delegation of greeters. It was a
quiet, low-pitched group of only three men. Not a challenge, but a statement of their presence, and an unspo-
ken question of the visitors: *Who are you, and what is
your purpose?* It was apparent that there was no threat
of conflict, because the newcomers had women and children with them. Still . . .

White Fox, flanked by his two sons, rode slowly toward
the three men. His right hand was raised, palm forward,
in the universal hand-sign: *See, I have no weapon. I come
in peace.* He reined his horse to a stop.

The man who appeared to be the leader returned the
sign, and stood staring for a moment, a puzzled look on
his face. Then he broke into a smile.

"Fox?" he asked. "White Fox? Get down, my brother!
It has been a long time!"

"Tall Corn? You have changed little!" White Fox replied, laughing.

"Nor have you!"

From that moment, the visit became a time of joyful
reunion. There was little language difficulty, except at
the level of Strong Bow's generation, which had had less
contact with the people of the pueblo. With the help of
hand-signs, even that progressed well.

"Is this your son, Red Horse?" their host asked, looking
at Strong Bow.

"No, no, this is our younger son," Fox explained. "He
was small when we last saw you."

"Of course! Then where is Horse?"

"Here, Uncle!" Red Horse laughed.

"Ah! *You* are Red Horse? But you are . . ." He paused,
and everyone chuckled. Tall Corn joined in the merri-

ment. ". . . are grown! And so is your brother. Ah, it *has* been a long time. Strong Bow, this one?" He glanced at the young man's height, broad shoulders, and well-muscled arms. "Yes, he is named well. But when you were last here, he was but a child, was he not?"

"That is true. It was ten, maybe twelve summers past," agreed White Fox. "And how are your people?"

Tall Corn nodded.

"It is good with us. The older ones say that the winters are harder here than at home in the southern mountains. But who knows? Winters *are* harder for the older ones."

"True. How do your crops grow here?"

"They do well, mostly. The land has a different spirit, it is said. Not better or worse, but different. There is more rain, they say. But of course that varies from one season to the next."

"Yes."

The conversation continued as they walked toward the village, a cluster of the square mud-brick lodges nestled in the shallow canyon. They were walking past patches of growing things that Strong Bow recognized, and some that he did not. Corn was easily identified, and pumpkins, and the vines that climbed on tripods of poles must be some sort of beans. Onions . . . yes, but there were several plots of plants that looked totally unfamiliar. Of course, he had never been around a village of Growers to any extent at this time of year. Or any time, actually. Nor did he want to, particularly.

There were people working in some of the patches, using a tool which appeared to be made from the shoulder blade of a buffalo, bound to a stick with rawhide. It was much like an ax, but the blade was placed at right angles to the handle . . . crosswise, instead of vertically. Odd, he thought, but then realized why. These people were using the tool to chop at the ground in front of them, removing some sort of undesirable plants. Occasionally, one would pause and reach to pull an offending growth out of the earth, knock the dirt from its roots, and then drop the plant to the ground.

Aiee, he thought, *what a way to spend one's days!* How much better to ride a good buffalo horse, with the wind in one's hair, in the excitement of the chase . . . But as his brother had said, fish swim, birds fly. To each his own.

They were among the lodges now. Children with large dark eyes peered cautiously at the newcomers.

"Come," called Tall Corn, "meet our kinsmen from the plains. Here, Basket Woman, you remember White Fox, our cousin. They have come to visit. We will have stories tonight, little ones! It is good!"

The warm days and cool, quiet nights were pleasant for Strong Bow. He was popular with the children, as many big, quietly cheerful men are, because he was kind to them. He was interested in the customs of these easygoing, pleasant people, so different from his own. Naturally curious, naturally tolerant, Strong Bow related well to nearly anyone, so he was well regarded by all. He did not speak of his lack of understanding for those who would prefer to hoe corn instead of chasing buffalo. That, he concluded, was their loss. If someone must hoe corn, let it be them, not himself.

It was somewhat like religion, he concluded. One should not disdain the beliefs or taboos of another. The People, for instance, did not kill or eat bears. After all, are they not like humans, walking sometimes on two legs? It would be virtually cannibalism! The Head Splitters, however, close allies of the People, enjoyed bear meat, used the fur as robes and ornaments, and proudly wore necklaces made of bears' claws. But the People thought none the less of their allies because of this difference. A friend among the Head Splitters had once spoken sympathetically to Strong Bow as they camped together, and the other chewed on dried bear meat.

"I am sorry I cannot share this. Or maybe you will try it?"

Both laughed.

"No, no. I have pemmican."

So this situation, here among the people of the pueblos, was much the same, he concluded. The corn, the rain, the water-spirits, and their private ceremonies, all were a part of their lives. He could not relate to these customs, any more than these people would understand the Sun Dance, and the religious significance of the return of the sun, the grass, and the buffalo.

Of course, the Sun Dance was open to any visitors who were interested. Head Splitters often attended, having no Sun Dance of their own. They were welcome, and sometimes participated in the invitational dance ceremonies. It was a flattering thing, to have their interest in the ceremonies of the People.

By contrast, these growers of corn, though many of their ceremonies and songs were public, reserved their most important rituals from view. Some, even, were restricted to the privacy of the kivas, where none but the Elders and the qualified men were permitted to enter.

And that was another thing. Why, he wondered, was there such a difference in the status of their women? Women of the People could speak in council, hold office, could have the gifts of the spirit. They could participate in most ceremonies. The Warriors' Dance, even, if they chose the warrior trail. It was seldom done, but *could* be. One of his kinsmen, Running Eagle, grandmother of Pale Star, was such a woman. Her prowess was told and retold in song and story.

These women could not even enter the kivas . . . He

wondered how his grandmother, Moon Flower, had made the adjustment to the life of the People when she married Red Feather. Ah, well, it was no matter. Fish swim, birds fly.

5

》》 》》 》》

They had been in the pueblo only a few days when the rumor came. More than a rumor, actually. A traveler who stopped overnight there carried the news.

A Spanish expedition, he related, had set out from Santa Fe, and was now heading this way.

"We had heard they were back in Santa Fe," Tall Corn agreed. "But what is their purpose?"

The visitor shrugged.

"I do not know. Who knows what purpose Spaniards have?"

It had been a generation since the bloody war, when all Spanish in New Mexico had been killed or driven out. Their return was of no concern to Tall Corn's people, for that was far away. But this . . .

"Is this a war party?"

"I do not know, my brother. I have not seen them. But there are said to be more than a hundred men, some with horses and weapons."

"Where are they now?"

"Maybe a few sleeps behind me. The Elders at a pueblo to the west asked me to tell you. The Spanish are stopping at each town."

"But *why?*"

The visitor shrugged again.

"They are behind me, not before, my brother, so I do not know. I hear only rumor."

"You said they are to the west?"

"Yes. They came across Raton and followed the eastern edge of the mountains north."

"Mm . . . our route, when we traded there," White Fox mused. "Who leads them?"

"Their chief is a Spaniard. But many of the party are our people."

There was a gasp of astonishment from the listeners.

"*Our* people?" Tall Corn asked incredulously. "People of the pueblos?"

"Yes! Who else?"

"But . . ."

It was an astonishing idea. If the people of the pueblos near Santa Fe were cooperating with the Spanish, they must have a working alliance. That seemed impossible, with all the ill will that had brought on the war.

"But Popé?" Tall Corn persisted. "He would not have dealt with the Spanish."

The revolution had been led by this holy man, whose disposition had certainly not been improved during his imprisonment by the Spanish. He had tried to destroy or drive out everything Spanish. This had seemed excessive to some of his own people, even while the war still raged. It seemed ridiculous to the frugal pueblo people to destroy all the useful things such as sheep, pigs, and metal tools. Word had filtered this far that Popé had lost much of his political prestige, and had become a tyrant. The people of this transplanted pueblo on the plains had given thanks for the insight of Blue Corn and their other

Elders. They had foreseen such a problem, and avoided
it by the move. Popé had finally been overthrown by his
own people, because of his tyranny.

"Surely you knew that Popé is dead," the visitor related.

"We heard such a story. But we get little news here,"
Tall Corn explained.

"Yes, years ago, before the Spanish returned."

"Ah! So long?"

"Yes . . . He recovered part of his power, but it was
never the same. Then he died, and the Spanish came
back."

"No one resisted?"

"Not really. You have to realize, brother, that the
Spanish are changed. They are much easier to live with
now."

"They do not try to tear down our religion?"

The visitor laughed.

"Well, yes, they do. But only with talk now. Their holy
men do not imprison and hang ours any more. They say
'do not worship in the kivas, do not make your spirit-
medicine,' but our people do it, and the Spanish look the
other way. Maybe they do not want another war!"

There were chuckles around the circle, but the tone of
the conversation remained serious.

"But," persisted Tall Corn, "no one knows why they
send this expedition to the plains?"

"Not really. As far as I have heard, they have harmed
no one. Maybe they seek to make peace. But who knows?
As I have said, they are behind me, so I have had no news
for several sleeps."

Tall Corn nodded. It was a puzzling thing.

Strong Bow was quite interested in this entire turn of
events. All his life, he had heard of the Spanish, and the
exciting journeys to their land. His father and grandfa-

ther had even been imprisoned by these people. Still, old Red Feather seemed to regard them with some degree of esteem. Some affection, even. Possibly, Strong Bow reasoned, these strange Spanish were much like other people. Some deserve respect and admiration, some do not.

And though most of the people of the pueblo seemed apprehensive about the approaching Spanish, he was rather stimulated by the excitement. He had long felt that it was his misfortune to have been born too late. All of the excitement and romance that his father's generation had lived; all the adventure of the generations before that . . . Even his brother Horse had lived a more exciting life, and had been involved in the restoration of the white buffalo cape of the People. By contrast, his own life was pretty boring. He had not really thought about it before, but nothing much had ever happened to enliven the youthful seasons of Strong Bow. He had grown up in a period of peace and prosperity. All of the glory days of the People were behind them. It had even been possible to travel here to visit relatives with no real threat of danger. Yes, everything was becoming commonplace now. He should have been born a generation ago, when there was still excitement and adventure.

But now there was at least the possibility of something now. Strong Bow had been stimulated to some degree by the new contacts, new sights, sounds, and smells, the new foods of the pueblo. Now he would experience firsthand the thrill of meeting, perhaps even talking with, the outsiders who had influenced the People so strongly. Their very name brought a thrill of excitement. *Spanish!*

"Do these Spanish use the hand-signs?" he asked Red Horse.

"Yes, some," his brother answered. "At least, that is what our father says. The French use more."

"French . . . You have seen them, Horse?"

"Yes, before you were born. Our father guided for them, and Mother and I went along. You have heard that story . . . their town on the Big River?"

"Of course. But I had never wondered if they used hand-signs."

"No matter . . . they are gone now."

"Gone where, Horse?"

"I do not know. Wherever they came from. Maybe they will come back someday. You know, some of our family were French."

"Aiee! Really?"

"Of course. A man called Sky-Eyes, because he had light eyes, though he could see. And Woodchuck . . ."

"He was French?"

"Yes! You did not know that? Well, no matter."

"But these Spanish, Horse . . . you did not see *them?"*

"No. But some of the People were caught in the war, when the Spanish went away. Some were killed. That is before my time. Our father was there, but only a young man."

"Yes, so I have heard. But what do you think they want now, Horse?"

His brother shrugged.

"Who can tell? We will know when they come."

Strong Bow nodded. His curiosity was reaching a high level.

"If they are doing no harm . . ." he began.

"But we do not know that," Red Horse interrupted. "Only that they had not, at the last that our traveler heard. Remember, my brother, these are the people who killed holy men, just for *being* holy men."

Their conversation was interrupted by a call from the direction of the pueblo.

"It is time to eat," observed Red Horse. "Come, they will wonder where we are."

The two rose, and walked along a well-worn path toward the buildings.

Strong Bow's thoughts were racing. The conversation had stirred his imagination. He had expected this summer's excursion to visit relatives to be only a pleasant, mildly interesting diversion. Instead, it now appeared that it could be one of the most exciting things he had ever experienced. Now he would no longer be the only one in the entire family to have not experienced the fascinating contact with strange outsiders from another world far away.

The "Metal People," those of the pueblos called them . . .

6
>> >> >>

The approaching caravan was quite impressive. Strong Bow had never seen so many horsemen at one time before, except at the annual Sun Dance. These, of course, were far more exciting. The brilliant colors worn by some of the Spanish were awesome to behold. Their weapons, too . . . long curved weapons that hung from the waists of some. Strong Bow could not think what those might be, but Red Horse told him they were long knives, carried in a scabbard.

"*Aiee,* a knife *that* long?"

"Yes. The French use them, too. Theirs are a little different."

The very thought of facing an opponent armed with such a weapon sent a chill up his back. A tightening sensation in the pit of his stomach spread to his flanks and groin.

About half, possibly more, of the approaching riders were natives, who appeared from their dress and hair to be men from the pueblos. They, too, were armed, but their demeanor was not threatening. To them, this seemed much like a reunion, an anticipated visit with some of their own people.

The colorful caravan moved along the rim of the shallow canyon at a quick, determined pace, and paused opposite the village. A man who appeared to be their leader rode forward at a walk, flanked by another Spaniard and a man of the pueblos. Strong Bow presumed that the latter would be an interpreter. The dress of the two Spaniards was similar, but that of the leader was somewhat more intricately decorated. Yes, this man carried himself like a chief, and the other must be one of his warriors.

"Greetings, my brothers," the interpreter began.

Tall Corn stepped forward, returning the sign for peace.

"Welcome," he offered. "You speak our tongue . . . Who are you, and who are these?"

The other man smiled.

"It is as I thought," he said. "We are looking for the pueblo of Blue Corn, an Elder of our people, who came this way, after the war."

"Who wishes to know?" Tall Corn was still suspicious.

The interpreter hurried to reassure him.

"We mean no harm, brother. I am a kinsman. Blue Corn is my uncle."

"And my father," added Tall Corn. "But Blue Corn is dead."

"Ah! We are relatives! It is good that we meet."

"But what of these Spanish?"

"Oh, do not worry . . . They are much different now."

Tall Corn still had doubts. He remembered the bloody tragedy of the war.

"They do not try to stop the ceremonies in the kivas?"

The other man chuckled.

"Well, they do not like it, but often look the other way."

The Spanish chief was shifting restlessly in the saddle, and now spoke to the interpreter. They conversed for a moment in the Spaniard's tongue, while the others waited. Then the interpreter turned back to Tall Corn.

"He wishes a council with you," he said. "This is the village he seeks."

Tall Corn nodded.

"Bid him welcome," he began. "Tell him that they may camp there, on the flat by the stream." He pointed. "We will hold council tonight."

"It is good. This Spanish chief is called Villasur . . . They have strange names, do they not? And may I tell him your name?"

"Tall Corn."

"Yes. A son of Blue Corn, whom we sought?"

Tall Corn was uncomfortable with this repeated attempt to identify him and the village.

"Tell me, brother," he demanded, "why is this important?"

"He will probably ask you to bring your people home. That is his mission. Or part of it, anyway."

"But this is our home now," protested Corn.

"So, we will tell him that. But let us do it properly, in council."

Everyone in the village was present that evening, when the last rays of the sun had disappeared. The lengthening shadows had finally melded together in the soft shades of twilight, and the council fire was lighted.

It was a ludicrous situation, unrecognized by most of those present. The pueblo people, easygoing and tolerant by nature, were now tense and a little hostile. Grim, angry expressions were seen on many faces. The Spanish, on the other hand, were also behaving in an uncharacteristic manner. Usually hard and domineering, they now approached the people of the village with friendly, placating smiles. All except the Spanish officer Villasur, of course. As military leader of the expedition, he seemed to feel the importance of maintaining his dignity. His was a cold, expressionless face, firm and professional.

During the late afternoon, the visiting natives had mingled with those of the village. Many found relatives, and there were joyful reunions. The visitors tried to reassure their kinsmen that things had changed since the return of the Spanish.

"They mean us no harm now," one man pleaded with the uncle whom he was meeting for the first time. "These Spanish are different."

"You are too young to remember," the old man responded. "A Spaniard is a Spaniard. These are the people who killed our kinsmen with the rope!"

It was the worst of all possible deaths, that by hanging. If the throat is tied shut, how can the spirit escape to cross over to the Other Side? It is trapped in a corpse.

"I know, Uncle, but that is not done now. They have been back in Santa Fe for several summers now, and there has been no trouble."

"Then why do they come with lances and long knives and many soldiers?"

That was harder to explain.

"Uncle, one does not travel unknown country unarmed."

"Well . . . we will see."

The crowd was quieting now, the fire growing to push back the thickening shadows. People were still shifting a little to find comfortable places to sit. Strong Bow settled in between his father, White Fox, and his brother. A cottonwood pole fell apart as the fire gnawed it in two, and the pieces fell into the coals. A shower of sparks flew skyward, to be lost among the myriad of heavenly sparks now scattered across the blackness of the sky. Strong Bow watched . . . It was still a thrill, to sit before a fire and watch it behave as a living thing. And a council fire, reaching toward the heavens to assist in reaching a union of spirits . . . ah, the only thing he had thought better, as a child, had been a story fire.

Now Tall Corn rose and delivered a formal welcome through the interpreter. Villasur replied, though more briefly. The interpreter, it seemed, tried to embellish his translation to make it somewhat more proper.

"The Spanish chief says he is honored to be here with his brothers of the pueblo. It makes his heart glad. The time is long overdue when our peoples become friends again."

The crowd was silent, a stony silence that grew for a few moments. At Strong Bow's elbow, his father gave a wry little chuckle. Time spent in a Spanish jail had not increased White Fox's regard for these people, even though that was long ago.

Tall Corn was speaking now.

"Why," he began cautiously, "does our brother come with many men and horses and weapons?"

The interpreter relayed the question, and Villasur spread his palms as if to indicate that the answer was obvious.

"He says there might have been enemies," the interpreter stated.

"We have no enemies. We trade with all. But no matter. What is his purpose here?"

After the clumsy pause for translation, the answer came back.

"To bring you home."

There was a little flutter of conversation, but it soon quieted.

"This *is* our home," Tall Corn said firmly. "We have been here for a generation now."

There was a momentary flare of anger in the face of the Spanish officer as the statement was translated. He gave a short, angry retort, and the interpreter, who appeared quite uncomfortable, apparently tried to soften it.

"He says that we can discuss that later," he relayed. "When we return, maybe."

"Return?"

"Yes. We go downriver from here."

"East?"

"Yes, that is what he has said."

"How far? There are no other pueblo people east of here."

That information was relayed to the officer, who had partly regained his composure now.

"He says he knows that," the reply came back, "but I am not sure that he did."

There were quiet chuckles.

"Why does he go east, then?"

After translation and reply, the answer came back.

"He seeks the French."

"French? There are none here."

"True. But he asks, are there French to the east?"

"We have seen none."

Again there was translation and discussion, and the interpreter turned again.

"Did not the French trade in Santa Fe?"

"Maybe . . ."

Tall Corn turned to White Fox.

"Do you know of this, my brother?"

Fox nodded.

"They once did."

"Are there French in your country?"

"No, not now."

"Then there were?"

"Not really in *our* country. Farther north, on the river they called the Platte."

The interpreter relayed this information and Villasur snapped a quick question.

"He asks, is this not the Platte? The stream just north of us here?"

"No, it is north, but maybe two sleeps from here," Tall Corn replied.

Villasur took that in disgruntled silence, but finally spoke, and his question was relayed.

"He says another river, north? Then who of you has been there?"

There was silence, and men looked from one to another. Then Villasur spoke again, through the interpreter.

"He wants someone to guide this party. We go on, to find the French."

7
» » »

Strong Bow was never certain afterward what had made him volunteer.

"But, my son, you do not know that country. You have never even been to the Platte," White Fox argued.

"That is true, Strong Bow," his brother warned. "How could you guide them?"

With such a challenge, he was obliged to justify his position. Also, he was a little angry at his family for their objections. When he had begun the argument, he was only lukewarm about the project. Now he was determined.

"It will be easy," Strong Bow insisted. "What is there to know? We will go straight north until we strike the Platte or one of its smaller streams, then follow it east."

"But there are other nations living there," his father said. "Pawnees, Mandans, maybe. You do not know them."

"Not well. But they use hand-signs, Father. I can talk to these Spanish through their pueblo man, Turtle's

Foot, and with those on the Platte with hand-signs. I can be very useful to them."

Finally Red Horse swung his opinion to the side of his brother.

"He is a grown man, Father. Let it be as he says. I was younger, on our trip with the French."

"True," White Fox admitted. "But you were with your parents."

"Yes, of course. But I was younger. As I have said, Strong Bow is a man. He can decide."

White Fox shrugged his shoulders and spread his hands in a gesture of defeat.

"Let it be so. I cannot tell a man which trail to choose."

South Wind was disturbed, of course, but after the expected preliminary scolding, she decided that protest was pointless. She had raised two headstrong sons, both of whom were much like their father.

For Strong Bow, the expedition now seemed the answer to all his need for excitement and adventure. Since he had never been to the area in question, there was no limit to his anticipation of the wonders he would see, the sights and sounds of strange and unfamiliar cultures. He wondered what some of the women might be like. Though he had not yet married, Strong Bow had a strong attraction to the opposite sex. He was certain that he was not destined to be a man-woman, like his boyhood friend Birdsong, or like old Calf-Tongue of the Eastern band. No, he had simply never found the woman for him. His childhood friends had paired off and established their own lodges, except for Birdsong, of course.

So, he found himself dreaming romantic daydreams of the exotic women he might encounter, of long well-shaped legs and smooth skins and dark, haunting eyes that smoldered with promise. Green, maybe. Mandan women were said to have green eyes. Sometimes, anyway. He had never seen anyone with green eyes, and could not easily imagine it. Maybe they would be something like the odd grayish-colored eyes of some of the People. Descendants of Sky-Eyes, it was said.

So, the decision was made and Strong Bow's services were accepted by the Spanish officer. Villasur was immediately impatient to push on. He continued to ask many questions about the French, which seemed odd, both to the People and to those of Tall Corn's pueblo. No French had been seen for years, by either group.

Strong Bow approached the interpreter.

"Why does your Spanish chief ask of the French so much?"

Turtle's Foot shrugged.

"Who knows? He has done that since we started. They are enemies, maybe."

"But our people say they once traded."

"That is true, the older ones say. I do not know."

"But why would they be enemies now?"

Turtle's Foot shrugged again.

"Something in their own country, where both came from, maybe. Do your people have enemies?"

"No, not really. We do not go too far east . . . the Forest People do not welcome us. We have had enemies in the past."

He remembered stories of the invasion by Blue Paints, many lifetimes ago, turned back by the joint effort of the People and the Head Splitters. Was it not that the Head Splitters, now allies, had once been enemies? Yes, that was the story. They had worked together to defeat a greater enemy. It might be the same for the Spanish and French . . . friends for a few generations, then enemies, then friends again. He mentioned his theory to Turtle's Foot, who merely shrugged as he answered.

"Who knows? The French may be as strange as the Spanish. They all look alike, and have strange names and strange ways."

Little more was said about Tall Corn's people and the wish of the Spanish that they return to New Mexico. Villasur left no doubt, however, that the matter would be considered when he returned.

So, the expedition set out, heading northeast across the upland prairie. Once they crossed the river, which the pueblo people called the Smoky, the going was good. There was game in plenty, and grass for the many horses. There were scattered bands of antelope, and a few of elk, but only occasional buffalo. Perhaps a bull and a couple of cows, or a pair of cows with their calves. Once there was a small herd, consisting of three or four old cows, their yearling offspring, and their calves of this season. All of these scattered buffalo, it was assumed, were individuals that had left the main herd during the migration to the northern plains. They had been left behind, choosing to remain in some favorable grazing spot rather than continue the dusty journey. If they survived without the protection from predators that the other thousands of individuals provided, they would probably rejoin the migration as it moved back southward in the autumn.

Meanwhile, these scattered animals provided meat for the expedition on the move. Turtle's Foot and Strong Bow would ride ahead of the main party and seek any quarry that opportunity offered. Strong Bow was more experienced in this sort of hunting, and managed to select the fattest and most tender of game. The other guide, too, and some of the younger of the pueblo men took a great interest, and the party was well supplied with meat.

There came a day when, late in the afternoon, they saw ahead a wandering line of trees, indicating the course of a stream.

"Is this the Platte?" Villasur asked, through Turtle's Foot.

"I am not sure," Strong Bow admitted. "Maybe not

. . . This stream does not seem big enough. And look
. . . it runs northeast."

"Then it is not the river we seek?" Villasur insisted.
Strong Bow shook his head.

"I think not," he told Turtle's Foot. "Tell him that the
Platte should lie almost due east and west, where we
strike it. It is said to be straight, also. This stream is as
crooked as a snake."

Turtle's Foot relayed the information, and Villasur
nodded, obviously displeased.

"This stream flows in our direction," Strong Bow offered. "If we follow it, we should come to the Platte."

"How far?" Villasur wanted to know, through the interpreter.

"I do not know. I have never been here, either. But
this stream will lead us to the river we seek."

"Why is he so eager for the Platte?" Strong Bow asked
Turtle's Foot that evening as they camped beside the
unknown stream.

Turtle's Foot shrugged in his characteristic way.

"I do not know, Strong Bow. He has been asking . . .
It is like his questions about the French. He asks everyone, since we started. I do not know why. Is there something special about the Platte?"

"No, I think not . . . It is a little north of my people.
There are Pawnee."

"And French?"

"No. Once, maybe. The French came into this area,
but then pulled back."

"Back?"

"Yes, to wherever they came from, I guess. It was
while the Spanish were gone from Santa Fe, maybe."

"Ah! Maybe that is it! The Villasur wants to find if there
are French on the Platte."

Strong Bow nodded.

"Maybe. Turtle's Foot, I think you are right. His people and the French are enemies now, and he wishes to know where they are!"

"Do you think they are here?"

"I do not know, Turtle. My people have not been on the Platte for a generation."

The two were silent for a few heartbeats.

"We will see," said Turtle's Foot.

"Yes, we will see."

8
>> >> >>

Pedro de Villasur stared across the rolling prairie at the flaming colors of the sunset. His thoughts were not on the land and its changeable moods, but on the coming campaign.

The expedition had done well, so far. They had traveled well, despite the lack of discipline among the half a hundred natives who had accompanied him from Santa Fe. It was frustrating, that lack of discipline. He was accustomed to having his orders obeyed, his demands met. Although rather inexperienced in military command, he was certain of one thing: A leader orders, and his followers carry out that order.

It had been frustrating, his appointment as Lieutenant Governor. There was honor to it, and he had been thrilled at first. But it was not long before he realized the deception. A lieutenant governor has little to do. All important decisions were made by the Governor. Lesser decisions were made by others, who reported to the Governor.

Of course, his position was partly governmental and partly military. A sort of hybrid, he had decided. And, unfortunately, as sterile as a hybrid. Like a mule, with no past and no future, he sometimes felt. His military responsibilities were largely ceremonial. Again, most of the decisions were made by others. The military decisions, in fact, were made by those *under* him. Assignments to barracks rosters, patrols, guard duties, all the unexciting routine of a frontier post.

Villasur had attempted to bring some sophistication to the garrison, with extra drill formations and inspections. His orders were obeyed, grudgingly and to the letter, but that was all. It had already become apparent that his efforts were useless by the time the Governor had suggested that the extra drill be discontinued, for the morale of the troops. This had left him again with nothing but the boredom of his job with no seeming purpose.

It had been exciting to be assigned charge of the expedition to the plains. There was the anticipation of action. His troops felt it, too, and responded almost enthusiastically to the prospect of adventure. And they merely thought it an exploring party. It had been decided not to mention the French until later. At the appropriate time, he would reveal the true purpose of the expedition. For, despite the Governor's statement of dual purpose, in the mind of Villasur, there was but one primary goal: to counter the French thrust into the plains.

Now he was becoming eager. Increasingly, he attached less importance to the contact with renegade pueblo villages. What if they did not return? What difference would it make? Let them stay, or go to hell, for all he cared.

This assignment was an exciting opportunity. Here he was actually in command, able to make decisions and have them carried out. He could *show* his leadership ability, and it had done wonders for his morale. The soldiers had traveled well, and discipline was at least acceptable. Except, of course, for the natives, who would probably never be really disciplined.

The policy in dealing with natives had changed now, since the return after the war. It was no longer considered good policy to try to force them to cooperate. That, it was said, had precipitated the war before. Villasur did not entirely agree with this policy. There were times, he was certain, that a proper course of action was firm control by strength. An iron fist, rather than the extended hand of peace.

Well, be that as it may. He would have loved to attack that ragtag pueblo back there, show them the edge of the sword, and order them to cooperate with the Governor's wishes. Yet he had been assigned to persuade, not force, any such groups he encountered. No matter. He would try more persuasion on the return trip, after he had explored the Platte.

And that possibility was the biggest thrill of all. After the Governor had told him of the mission, Villasur had carefully studied the report of the Tejas incident. He could surmise from the incomplete, secondhand description in the letter to the Governor that there had been a hot little skirmish. Of course, to the participants, no engagement is a "little" event. Spanish troops had been attacked by a French unit "and their native allies" in East Tejas, the letter had said.

This appeared serious. Many of the tribes were quite warlike, unlike the pueblo people. These were hunters and fighters, skilled in the use of weapons. There had never been much friction with them, but the present situation appeared different. With France and Spain at war at home, it was quite like the French to enlist natives to do their fighting. Had they not done the same to the English farther north?

From that point on, it was easy to see the possibilities

and the threat to Spain. Natives all across the continent, perhaps, well armed and led by French officers skilled in military tactics . . . This could be a very serious threat to Spain's territorial claims. It was a matter so serious, in fact, that he and the Governor had decided to keep that part of the mission a secret. The others would know only that they sought renegade pueblo people from New Mexico, to induce them to return.

The critical nature of this secret mission did not sit lightly on the shoulders of Pedro de Villasur. In his own mind, at times, he could visualize himself as the leader of a small but determined force who would save the continent for Spain. To do so, of course, would require superhuman effort against incredible odds. They would fight to the last man, if need be, holding back the savage hordes in the name of the Crown. And he, Pedro de Villasur, would lead them.

Having allowed himself this romanticized version of the situation, he had only to fill in the gaps. By this time, he had nearly forgotten that his mission was to seek and report the status of the French on the Platte. Now, with a sense of deep conviction, the question in his mind was no longer whether the French were active on the Platte. The question was, *how many* French? He was completely certain that on this expedition, he would encounter hostile natives, stirred up and led by French officers. Some of these French dogs might be skilled tacticians, and it would be his privilege to match wits with them. Sometimes he could hardly wait.

Still, he wished to be prudent. That was the reason for his recruitment of the young native from the plains. He would show the French that he, too, could play their game. Strong Bow, the man was called, it was said, in his own strange tongue. Much of the communication with this man seemed to be with hand-signs. Very useful, those hand signals. Someday, Villasur told himself, he

would learn to use them. But for now, it was enough.
Strong Bow could provide information through the interpreter as to the general terrain, the tribes they might
encounter, and could make inquiry regarding the
French. Villasur was not yet certain whether to trust his
guide, but he would see. If the man became a problem,
he would have him killed. So far, he had no major suspicions. It had been curious, of course, that Strong Bow
had chosen this stream, on which they now traveled, as
the one they wanted. They had crossed many streams
since they left the pueblo, some quite small, others
nearly this wide. The guide had not even considered any
of them as a tributary of the river they sought.

Why? Strong Bow professed never to have seen this
territory before, yet insisted with certainty about the
stream. Maybe the ones they had crossed previously *had*
followed a slightly different direction. It was true that
they were heading northeast in following this one, but
Villasur hated to be in doubt. He was still unsure that he
could trust the guide. Why had Strong Bow volunteered
to lead them? He seemed amiable and harmless enough,
and had been traveling with the older couple who may
have been his parents.

But, suppose, now . . . Would that not be an excellent cover for a French spy? Strong Bow could have
approached as if in all innocence and arranged to lead
them wherever he chose. Actually, he was doing just
that. He could be leading them into a French stronghold.
He did keep denying all knowledge of the French, which
seemed unlikely. The man was skilled with weapons, too.
Did this indicate military experience with the French?

Villasur would have inquired more deeply into the
matter, and discussed it with his interpreter, except for
one thing. He did not trust Turtle's Foot, either. He was
so firmly convinced in his own mind that there were

French on the Platte . . . Was the river not *named* by them? They must be there.

By this line of reason, every action of their guide became suspect. He was leading the party straight into a French stronghold, while still protesting that he had never been here before. Villasur was pleased that he had been able to reason out the situation. He would not be caught unaware. At the slightest hint of trouble, he would personally shoot the treacherous guide. He was more certain each day that the guide was intentionally leading them directly toward the French strength. At least, where the French were assumed to be.

In his inexperience, suspicion, and distrust, Pedro de Villasur was overlooking one major fact: Strong Bow was doing exactly what he had been *asked* to do.

9
>> >> >>

It was a village unlike any that Strong Bow had ever seen. The first inkling of the difference was the appearance of the dwellings themselves. At first they appeared quite low, not high enough to stand in. That would be unusual for this sort of lodge, he thought. They were built of logs or some similar construction, with earth banked up and over the sides and roof. Then he realized that they must be half buried in the ground.

Of course, he thought. He had heard of the earthsheltered lodges of the Pawnee, and this must be what they looked like. More like a mound or hillock than a lodge, especially when viewed from any other angle than the doorway.

They had reached this stream two sleeps ago, and identified it as the Platte. At least, Strong Bow thought it was. He could not be absolutely certain, and there was no one in the entire party who had ever seen the Platte. But it must be. There was no other river of similar size in this area, as far as he knew.

Villasur was elated.

"Are you sure?" he asked through the interpreter.

"Not completely," Strong Bow admitted. "I am as sure as one can be, with not having seen it before."

"But how do you know?"

It was difficult enough trying to converse through the interpreter. Even more difficult was the task of trying to explain the feel for the spirit of a place. This was something that had puzzled the People before. Strong Bow remembered that his father had spoken of this. The Spanish, and the French, too, it was said, somehow failed to recognize things of the spirit. It was a defect, some thought. At the time of Creation, maybe . . . those nations from the hairfaced part of the world had simply failed to receive the knowledge of spirit. It would have been amusing, if it were not so tragic, not to know spirit-things. And how ironic, the most tragic of all: The hairfaces thought that the Great Spirit had never before spoken to anyone but them!

So, how was it possible to tell someone with such limitations how to identify the stream they sought? This is the stream because it *feels* like its spirit. To explain such things . . . *aiee*, one might as well try to explain to the Spanish how he knows North or East.

But now, Strong Bow's impression had apparently proved correct. They had found the Pawnees. At least, one band. The Pawnees were said to be a far-flung nation. But contact with this band indicated that this was the proper area.

Strong Bow was quite pleased, of course. He had sensed a distrust on the part of the Spanish leader, Villasur. There were too many questions, too many sidelong glances. At first he had thought it only the mark of a good leader, one who notices everything. He soon realized, however, that it was not that. It was something else . . . The leader was watching *him*, Strong Bow. And watching with an intensity, a constant . . . a *suspicion!* Yes, that was it. Why, he wondered. Had Strong Bow done something to merit this distrust? He spoke to Turtle's Foot about it.

"I do not know," the interpreter admitted. "He does not trust me, either. Maybe he trusts no one."

"It is sad," Strong Bow observed. "He must be very lonely."

Turtle's Foot shrugged.

"That is his problem."

"Yes . . . but to have no one to trust . . . *aiee!*"

Now, however, as they approached the village, Villasur seemed to have forgotten his suspicions, at least temporarily. His eyes were bright with excitement as they rode forward.

"We should stop here and wait," said Strong Bow to the interpreter when they were two or three bow shots from the nearest lodges.

"Why?"

"It is custom. It says we do not want to attack."

Despite this, they could now see armed men moving in the fringe of trees, deploying along the slope in defensive array. The Southern band of the People, far away from their neighbors to the north, seldom encountered Pawnees. As far as he could remember, Strong Bow had never seen men of this nation. Their appearance, then, was something of a shock. On each man's head there appeared a hat or headdress of some sort, standing erect . . . No! It was not a hat . . . *Aiee!* Did they have *horns?* A single projection jutted up and forward, like a slightly curved horn, from the top of each man's head.

There was a gasp from Turtle's Foot at his side.

"Horns?" he echoed the question Strong Bow had just asked himself.

"We call them Horn People," Strong Bow admitted, "but . . ."

He had always assumed that this descriptive term referred to their use of buffalo horn for spoons and rattles, as other nations used that material. His thoughts were whirling. Then he realized with amusement . . . The *hair* had been plastered and shaped and pulled to a long point to appear this way. With tallow and paint, probably . . . This unexpected appearance would certainly startle the enemy, as it had this party.

Villasur was firing rapid questions at Turtle's Foot.

"Tell him it is their hair," Strong Bow advised.

The horned warriors were now advancing, cautiously but not in fear. The Spanish party, counting their pueblo allies, appeared to outnumber the fighting men of this band, though not greatly. Still, it would be well, thought Strong Bow, not to appear too aggressive. He raised his hand in the sign for peace. A man in the advancing line, who appeared to be a leader, raised an answering hand, and then continued to sign.

"How are you called?"

Strong Bow, who had the most knowledge of hand-signs, answered for the party.

"I am Strong Bow, of the Elk-dog People. These are visitors from far away."

The other man appeared suspicious.

"French?"

"No, another hairfaced people. Do you know of the Spanish, to the southwest?"

"We have heard. Your people trade with them?"

"Not now. We did."

"Who are these others?" he demanded, gesturing toward Turtle's Foot.

"Mud-lodge people."

"How is it that you are with them?"

Strong Bow was becoming impatient with all this suspicion.

"I speak for them," he explained. "In their country

hand-signs are seldom used. Besides, my brother, they are the people of my grandmother."

The horned leader nodded, somewhat pacified.

Villasur was fidgeting impatiently.

"Ask him what we wish to know," he demanded through the interpreter.

Strong Bow nodded.

"We are just beginning to calm their doubts," he told Turtle's Foot. "Tell him to be patient."

Turtle's Foot relayed that message, and Villasur sighed irritably. *Aiee,* thought Strong Bow, why were these hairfaces so impatient? Maybe it was part of their having not received the things of the spirit.

"It would be best," he said to Turtle's Foot, "if we wait until later to ask these things. Tonight, maybe, at a story fire. Ask him."

While that exchange was taking place, he turned back to the Pawnee, who was also becoming impatient now.

"Forgive me, my brother," he signed. "Our leader does not understand the hand-signs, so we must explain to him. Now, may we camp near you, maybe have story fires tonight? We move on tomorrow."

The grim-faced Pawnee, still not entirely convinced, hesitated for a little while, then nodded agreement.

"It is good."

He pointed to an area near the village.

"Water there, camp over there."

Villasur was insistently talking to Turtle's Foot, and the interpreter turned to Strong Bow.

"He still wants to know about the French."

It was a reasonable request, Strong Bow had to admit. If one suspects that an enemy may be in the area, he would wish to know before he camps. He turned back to the Pawnee.

"Our chief asks, are there French here?"

The horned warrior was quiet for a moment, then signed cautiously.

"Why does he wish to know?"

This was a politically delicate situation. If these Pawnees were allies of the French, it would not do to declare that the Spanish were enemies. That would be a foolish thing, to walk into such a village and announce yourself an enemy.

On the other hand, suppose that the Pawnees and French were enemies to each other? It would be equally foolish to declare friendship with the French.

Strong Bow thought rapidly. He wished that he had paid more attention to his father's stories of the French fort and their exploring expedition on the river. Was there not hostility on the part of the Pawnees? Or only some of them? *Aiee* . . .

Very carefully he began to sign, trying to appear as casual as possible.

"It is nothing. They are neighbors, back in their own land. Our leader only wondered."

It was plain, from the look on the face of the horned Pawnee, that he did not believe this explanation. His reply, too, was very cautious, and he, too, was trying to be very casual.

"We know of French," he signed. "We have seen none for a long time. Now, make your camp, and we will talk, later."

Strong Bow relayed this answer and Villasur merely grunted. They reined toward the designated camping area, Villasur muttering to himself.

"What did he say?" asked Strong Bow.

Turtle's Foot appeared uncomfortable.

"He said, 'He lies.' "

Now Strong Bow was uncomfortable.

"Who lies?"

"I do not know, my friend. Maybe the horned man, maybe you."

Strong Bow's anger flared, and he started to speak, but Turtle's Foot silenced him with a wave.

"Maybe me, even. He was speaking to himself."

"Turtle," said Strong Bow, "this could be very dangerous. No one trusts anyone."

"That is true," Turtle's Foot said glumly. "I think you and I have to trust each other."

10
>> >> >>

Despite the suspicion, it was a pleasant evening. Story fires were little different here, Strong Bow observed. He enjoyed the storyteller of the Horn People, an old man with a flair for the dramatic. Strong Bow had grown up with a storytelling tradition in the family. Pale Star, a relative of an earlier generation, was still revered as the greatest of storytellers, even after her death. So Strong Bow had seen many experts and their work at the story fires.

Rarely, however, had he seen skill that could even approach that of this man. The entire audience was spellbound by the setting, the clever choice of background, and the mixture of firelight, shadow, and moonlight that had been contrived to bring the narrative to life. The storyteller spoke and used hand-signs as well, which Strong Bow relayed to the other visitors through Turtle's Foot.

The Creation story of the Horn People, it seemed, was

somewhat similar to that of Strong Bow's own. They had come from inside the earth.

"First Man," the storyteller intoned, "was an old man already when he crawled out. In one hand he carried fire and a medicine pipe, in the other, a small drum to use in making music for the songs.

"Next came a woman, carrying a sack of seeds . . . corn, mostly, but a few pumpkin seeds."

Aiee! thought Strong Bow. The Horn People have been growers since Creation?

He had always heard of their fighting ability. Somehow this did not seem appropriate. Most of the Growers he had seen were quite nonviolent. He had linked these characteristics in his mind, assuming that those whose nature is that of growing are peaceable. After all, they must trade for other commodities . . . robes, meat . . .

He had also assumed, apparently incorrectly, that growers were virtually helpless against destruction of their crops by others. These Horn People gave the strong impression that any threat of violence would quickly be repaid in kind. The warriors he saw appeared quite capable of carrying out such a vendetta.

The horned storyteller paused, waiting for the visitors to take part in the evening's entertainment. Nothing happened, and there was a clumsy interlude, which became more and more uncomfortable. Strong Bow turned to Turtle's Foot.

"What is it? You do not wish to answer with your story? I will interpret."

Turtle's Foot shook his head.

"No. My people do not tell our Creation story . . . not like this."

Yes, Strong Bow remembered now. His grandmother's people had never participated in the story fires, except as observers. It was their choice, of course, a personal thing. If it was part of their complicated religion, and they wished *not* to share it, so be it. But in this case, a response to the storyteller of the Horned People was expected. Not to do so would be very rude.

"Will the Spanish tell theirs?" he asked quickly.

Turtle's Foot shook his head.

"No, I think not."

"They do not wish to tell one?" Strong Bow asked. "They can tell you, and I will change it into hand-signs for them."

"No, it is not that. The storytellers of the Spanish— their holy men, you know—they wish only to tell *their* story, not listen to others."

"Theirs is not a good story?"

"Oh, yes! Very good. They have a bad god who turns into a snake, and a poison fruit . . . One of their gods is half human, and is killed and comes back to life. A good story!"

Strong Bow was puzzled.

"Then why do they not tell it?"

"They do! They love to tell it all the time. But they want nobody else to tell another story. Tonight the Horn People told theirs, so the Spanish holy men refuse to come."

Strong Bow looked around. It was true. He had not realized . . . None of the three holy men in Villasur's party was present. It was a strange . . . yes, a rude and insulting thing, to refuse to listen to another's story. Another thought occurred to him.

"What about the other man? The one who speaks the French tongue?"

There was in Villasur's party a man who would be useful only if they encountered the French. He could speak both French and Spanish, and could act as interpreter if needed.

"Not him, either," Turtle's Foot explained. "He is not a

storyteller. Not even a holy man. They have the same story, anyway . . . same god."

"You mean, French and Spanish?"

"Yes. You did not know that?"

Strong Bow was now more confused than ever.

"No . . . They have the same Creation story, but are not the same?"

"I am told this," Turtle's Foot shrugged. "I do not understand either."

But now the Horn People were becoming restless, under the rudeness of the visitors. Someone must do *something*. Strong Bow rose to his feet, and addressed the old storyteller with great formality, using his own tongue and hand-signs.

"Forgive us, Uncle. Your story has been a good one, and we will reply. But we . . . I did not know that our leader's people do not trade stories. Also, that these others, my grandmother's people, do not. It is a thing of their medicine. Different spirits . . ."

The horned storyteller was nodding in understanding, but now Villasur was demanding, through Turtle's Foot, to know what was going on.

"Tell him," Strong Bow snapped, "that it is courteous to reply with a story. I am trying to do that."

He turned back to the fire.

"My friends, I am called Strong Bow," he began. "Mine are people called Elk-dog People by some."

There were nods of understanding.

"You may have heard of us, your neighbors to the south."

More nods, not entirely unfriendly.

"I will tell our story, that of my people," Strong Bow went on. "In the beginning . . ."

"The Villasur says ask about the French," Turtle's Foot interrupted.

"Tell him *later!*"

Now the storyteller reentered the conversation.

"What is it?" he inquired.

"It is nothing, Uncle. They do not understand the way of the story fires."

The old man shook his head sadly.

"Too bad."

"Yes. Now, as I said, the story of my people is much like yours. We were inside the earth, and crawled out through a hollow cottonwood log into the world. One of our god-beings sat on it and tapped with a stick. Each time he tapped, another came out of the log."

He paused a moment, wondering whether to use the joke. It was a tradition, to wait for some listener to ask . . . but that was during a friendly visit. The atmosphere here was tense, strained. For a good story, the listeners must *like* the storyteller, and be relaxed, pleased with him and his tales. Here, Strong Bow felt that *neither* group really trusted him, the Horn People or those with whom he traveled. The one who came closest was probably Turtle's Foot, who was also distrusted.

Just then, the old storyteller spoke again.

"Tell us, Elk-dog man, are your people still coming out of the log?"

Strong Bow was astonished. He looked into the old man's eyes and saw an unmistakable twinkle. The man *knew*. He had heard this story before, and could see that Strong Bow was in trouble. This was a storyteller trying to help a fellow storyteller.

"No, Uncle," Strong Bow answered solemnly. "Soon, a fat woman got stuck in the log, and no more have come through. That is why ours has always been a small nation."

There was an appreciative wave of laughter, and the Pawnee storyteller smiled, pleased at the outcome. Strong Bow nodded to him in appreciation. The old man caught his eye and nodded in answer.

The stories progressed, more smoothly now, but there was still something in the air that Strong Bow found unsettling. It was something he could not define, a spirit of distrust, somehow. It was not helped by the fact that Villasur kept insisting that they inquire about the French. Finally, he managed to do so, and received a quick answer.

"He says there are no French in the area," Strong Bow relayed to Turtle's Foot. "At one time, yes, but not now."

"Do you believe him?" the other asked.

"Yes. This is as my people know it. There was a town . . . the French . . . far east of here. My brother was there, with my father. But the French moved on."

Turtle's Foot nodded, but seemed lost in thought for a moment before he answered. Finally he sighed, and spoke.

"You know, my friend, that our leader will not believe this?"

Strong Bow nodded.

"That is true."

"Then what shall we tell him?"

Strong Bow shrugged.

"Tell him the truth. We do not make things as they are."

"Of course not. But . . ."

"Tell him what the Pawnee said, what I said. We can do no more."

There was a heated discussion between Villasur and Turtle's Foot, occasionally interrupted by the French-speaking interpreter. Finally Turtle's Foot turned back to Strong Bow.

"It is as we thought. He does not believe any of it."

"But both have heard the same thing . . . the Pawnee and I!"

"Yes, that adds to his suspicion. He is sure that the

Pawnees are in league with the French, and you are working with them."

Strong Bow was astonished.

"Why? Why would I do that? I have never seen these Horn People before!"

Turtle nodded.

"Yes, I believe you. But the Villasur is untrusting. I think he wants there to be French, so he sees everything in that way."

"But what does his French-talker say?"

Turtle's Foot chuckled, but there was no humor in it.

"What would you say, if you were the French-speaker? If there are no French, he has no use. They do not need him."

It had seemed such a simple thing, this exploring party. A pleasant, safe trip to see new country, new people. Strong Bow had not counted on the political intrigue, the distrust. He was somewhat offended that his word was not believed. Yet even worse was the danger that this represented. For a little while, he considered leaving. He could simply mount his horse and ride away. But that, of course, would only assure Villasur that his suspicions had been right. Besides, if he were to try it and be caught, he would be killed without hesitation. It was becoming a very dangerous situation.

He saw the French-talker eyeing him suspiciously, and wondered about the motives of that one. Grimly, he realized that he, Strong Bow, would be considered a danger by this man, no matter what the man's motives might be. He also realized how helpless he would be against the French-talker's treachery, if it came to that. A knife in the ribs while he slept . . . *Aiee*, his neck hairs bristled at the thought.

The story fire was low now, the sleepy people shuffling off to their beds. Strong Bow found himself next to the old Pawnee storyteller for a moment. The man spoke to him, quietly and quickly. More remarkably, in Strong Bow's own tongue.

"Be careful, Elk-dog man. There is danger!"

Strong Bow was so startled that it took a moment to collect his thoughts.

"Thank you, Uncle," he blurted, but the man was gone.

Strong Bow lay sleepless in his robe for a long time, trying to make sense of the whole thing. Here was a Pawnee, an old man who spoke the tongue of the People, and knew their Creation story. That in itself was easily explained. The man had spent some time in contact with the People, probably the Northern band.

But the warning of danger? This Pawnee could not know the dangers of political intrigue in Villasur's party. Therefore, he must be warning of something else, something ahead of them. But *what?* Could it be that Villasur's suspicion was true, that there *were* French in the area, plotting against the Spanish? That was the only explanation which occurred to Strong Bow.

It would have concerned him even more if he had seen the hard-riding horseman, some distance to the east. His horn-shaped scalplock was powdered with the dust of travel. The man paused to rest his horse, remounted, and hurried on. His goal was the next Pawnee town, downstream, and he had important information about the Spanish party.

11
>> >> >>

Lieutenant Governor Villasur was completely unaware of the messenger who had left the village so hurriedly after darkness fell. Still, he sensed that something was amiss. He had noted the exchange of glances between the Pawnee storyteller and the guide he had enlisted at the pueblo. He already distrusted the man, and now had evidence of some secret between him and the Pawnees.

Villasur was somewhat insulted that they would think him so gullible as to believe their blatant lies. No French in the area, indeed! His intuition told him a different story, which was supported by the French renegade, Le Boeuf. Of course, Villasur did not trust him, either. A man who is a traitor to his own kind is likely to be a traitor to his new masters also. But the Frenchman's story supported Villasur's theories. There *were* French on the Platte, in league with the Pawnees and this scoundrel from the other tribe who used hand-signs. *I must learn that skill,* he promised himself.

But for now . . . He toyed with the idea of killing the man. Strong Bow, he was called, in the strange naming customs used by the savages of the plains. *No*, he thought, *it will be more interesting to toy with him a bit.* Now that he had verified his suspicion of treachery, it would be amusing to watch the man's actions.

At the present time, all the versions pointed to similar information: There was another Pawnee village a day's travel down the Platte. Villasur suspected that there might be French officers there, and this view was supported by his French turncoat. It was denied strongly by the Pawnees and by their guide, Strong Bow, which strengthened Villasur's belief that they were all in league with the French. Possibly, even, the interpreter from Santa Fe, Turtle's Foot . . . *Another odd name*, he thought. Turtle's Foot, however, was now insisting strongly that he did not know anything about the area or the French, or anything else. *He knows that I suspect him*, thought Villasur. *He tries to save his own worthless skin.*

Well, he would watch that one. When the time came to make the decision, they could kill that one, too. Or not. Whatever seemed best.

They moved out the next morning, traveling downstream. The troops looked fairly competent, only a trifle inept at maintaining straight lines in military formation He would resume the close-order drill formations when they returned to Santa Fe. The natives, of course, were as undisciplined as ever. *Mother of God*, Villasur muttered to himself, *when can I have a command worthy of my ambitions?*

It was a good day for travel, though a trifle muggy. By noon Villasur was uncomfortable, his body damp with sweat. He longed for the cool shade of the adobe buildings in Santa Fe. The dusky interiors of the government structures were insulated from the sun's rays by thick walls which always felt cool to the touch. Here there was no shelter except the thin layers of his clothing. The heat of the burning sun could easily be felt through his tunic and shirt.

He called a rest stop, and the troops sought the thin shade of scrubby willows along the river. All too soon, it was time to move on.

As Villasur mounted and rode into the open, he glanced back to satisfy himself that his troops were looking lively. Or, if not lively, that they were observing the commands to remount and prepare to travel. It was only then that he noticed the clouds to the northwest. Scattered cottonlike tufts of white shone against the pure blue of the prairie sky. They were few and far between. *A pretty sight,* he thought. There were some things a man could actually enjoy about the appearance of this open sky and flat landscape.

Some time later, he felt a sudden relief from the burning rays of the sun, and glanced up, curious as to the cause. One of the drifting puffs of cloud was obscuring the sun for a moment, and he rode in shade. The patch of shadow was perhaps a hundred paces across, and moving rapidly. In a few moments, it had moved on, leaving him exposed once more to the beating rays of the sun. How nice it would be, he mused, if such a shadow could be found that moved in their direction of travel, and at the same speed. He looked across the distant landscape, and saw that the plain was now dotted with such shaded spots, all moving eastward. Was this odd phenomenon peculiar to prairie country? Or was it only noticed here because of the vastness of the plains, the distances that one could see?

Before long, he noticed that the cloud shadows were larger and more numerous. At the same time, there was a change in the wind. He was not certain what sort of change at first. The breeze had been from the south, hot and steady, though light, for several days. Now it seemed undecided, tentative, quiet for a few moments, then a puff of wind that came and was gone. The direction of the breeze seemed to be changing, too; now from the north, now west.

He watched a stray zephyr lift dust in a miniature whirlwind only a few hundred paces to their north. It grew, whirling in a giddy dance, becoming taller, taking a zigzag course across the flat plain like a living thing. Then, as suddenly, it was gone. Where the whirling rope-like thing had been, there was nothing. He had an eerie feeling, a premonition, that he could not explain. He glanced around to see if anyone else had been so affected.

Turtle's Foot caught his glance and smiled.

"Storm spirits," the interpreter said simply.

Villasur only nodded, trying to appear confident, as if he saw such things frequently. He was irritated that the man had caught him off guard. Hopefully, his curiosity about the odd little trick of the wind had not been interpreted as weakness. The column moved on.

By late afternoon, there was a heavy bank of dark gray clouds to the northwest, which seemed to be approaching more rapidly. Villasur decided that it would be prudent to call a halt for the day, to allow preparation of the camp before the storm struck.

"We will camp here," he announced, indicating a level area near the river.

A smaller stream, barely a trickle now in the heat of summer, joined the river here. The river itself was unimpressive, a narrow ribbon of water in a broad expanse of sand. They had discovered, however, that the sand was treacherous. It had the appearance of firm ground, but in some areas was actually soft and bottomless. One of the troopers had ridden his horse into such a spot, only to become mired in the sucking sand. The creature's strug-

gles only pulled it deeper. It had required men and
horses pulling with ropes to extricate the animal. Since
that incident, the column had taken care to avoid the
sandy river bed.

But the flat he had chosen for the camp was solid
ground. It was near enough to obtain water for men and
horses. Yes, a good camp site, he told himself. He was
completely surprised, then, when Turtle's Foot approached him with concern.

"Strong Bow says, not camp here."

"I will decide," Villasur snapped. "What does he
want?"

He was suspicious. He had already determined that
Strong Bow had a traitorous relationship with the Pawnees. But now the man was trying to control where they
camped. Was this the time? Would they be attacked by
French-led Pawnees at this camp? Maybe it was time to
kill the traitor.

"He says," Turtle's Foot continued, "that there will be
much water here. The river . . . this wide!"

The interpreter pointed to areas well outside the river's sandy bed. The flatness of the sandy plain was broken here by low banks, parallel to the stream bed itself.
Such a width, over a hundred paces, would put the selected camp site under water.

"I do not believe that," snorted Villasur. "He has some
treachery in mind."

"Señor," Turtle's Foot said seriously, "I would listen to
him. He is a man of country like this. He knows how the
water-spirits behave in his own country."

Villasur was angry now.

"No! He wants us to camp where it is easier to attack
us."

Turtle's Foot heaved a deep sigh.

"Señor, I think not." He pointed to a slight rise to the

north of the stream bed. "There, away from the river.
And maybe better from attack, anyway."

Villasur studied the situation for a moment. It was
true, the rise was probably more defensible. That was his
reason for the change in plans.

"Move away from the stream bed," he shouted. "We
will camp on the rise."

There was a lot of grumbling on the part of the
soldiers. It would be farther to walk for water. The natives seemed to accept the decision more easily. Villasur
was not entirely convinced that he had done the right
thing. It was inexcusable to let these ignorant savages
make his decisions. It was only coincidence, he assured
himself, that the slope might be more defensible than
the area he had chosen. And he was only half convinced
about the danger of flooding. In this arid plain, how
could there be a flood? No matter. If there was treachery
afoot, he would be ready. He posted extra guards.

It was just before dark that the storm struck. They
watched it come, the looming clouds laced with finger-
like displays of lightning, flickering networks of white
fire within the cloud bank. The roll of thunder was almost constant. He could see the bluish smear of falling
rain some distance away, heavier in some areas, lighter
in others. Incredibly, through openings in the storm, he
could see the distant plain and the orange of the sunset
sky.

The storm came closer, and the wind whipped into a
frenzied thing, driving the first patter of raindrops
against his face. He sheltered himself with a blanket as
the full force of the storm swept over them. He could see
nothing, beyond the driving black downpour. He noticed a change in the sound of the deluge, and saw
chunks of ice falling, bouncing crazily. Some were as
large as a small egg, though most were only the size of
marbles. The horses were fighting their tethers, lunging

at the unknown stinging things that peppered their un-protected backs and rumps. He saw one horse that had broken loose, running wildly, unable to escape the slash-ing sting of the hailstones. One of the larger stones struck Villasur a glancing blow on the knuckles, exposed as he held the blanket. He thought for a time that the hand might be broken, but the ache finally began to subside.

The rain and hail ceased as suddenly as they had come, and the thunder began to withdraw into the distance. The sound was replaced by another, a roaring, continu-ous rumble which seemed to come from the west. He tried to identify the sound. Running buffalo, startled by the storm? No, it lacked the earth-shaking quality.

A flash of lightning illuminated the area for a moment, and he gasped in astonishment. The river was a rushing torrent, out of its banks. Even in the brief flicker of light, he could see what appeared to be a wall of water, rolling downstream toward them. The next flash verified his impression. The narrow ribbon of the river was now easily a hundred paces wide. His chosen camp site was a frothing swirl of water.

So, his guides had been right. Their advice had saved his command. No matter. He still did not trust them. They were only interested in saving their own miserable lives. And probably, the time was not yet right for the attack by the French. That would come later, and he would be ready.

12
>> >> >>

The river was wider here, with more trees along its banks. The country was greener, with more of the familiar tall grasses and fewer areas of short, curly buffalo grass. Strong Bow was feeling more at home here, in surroundings more nearly like the Tallgrass Hills of the People.

They had encountered two more villages of Pawnees, but Villasur had insisted that they pause only long enough to ask questions about the French. He seemed to have resented the traditional stopover and social activities with story fires. That was a thing that Strong Bow could not understand.

Villasur's distrust had increased, too. He was now sending scouts ahead of the column, at least a day's journey in advance. It was obvious to Strong Bow that he, as the person most familiar with the country and the hand-signs, should be among the scouts. However, Villasur forbade it. Those who were sent ahead were soldiers, by twos and threes, accompanied by a pueblo native or two.

Even Turtle's Foot was not allowed to go with the advance scouts.

"I have become too friendly with you!" he joked to Strong Bow.

It was a hollow joke.

"I do not understand," Strong Bow mused. "What is it, that he does not trust me?"

"Who knows?" Turtle's Foot shrugged. "But I think it is dangerous. Maybe you should leave."

"That would not be right, Turtle. I have agreed to help them."

"True. But see how he looks at you? I think he means to kill you. You must be careful."

"I will, my brother, but I think you make this bigger than it is. If I am in danger, so are you!"

"Yes. We must look out for each other."

There came an evening when excitement rippled through the camp. Voices rose, and men were checking their weapons.

"What is it?" Strong Bow asked his friend.

"The scouts have reported a great force of Pawnees ahead."

"But we have seen Pawnees before."

"Their towns, yes. This is said to be different. Maybe Villasur thinks that here he will find the French."

This proved to be an accurate guess. The leader called everyone together, and made an announcement.

"Our scouts have observed a large gathering of Pawnee warriors, a day's travel ahead of us. Everyone must be alert. We will move rapidly, and make contact to see how many of the heretical Huguenots are with them."

"What is he saying?" whispered Strong Bow.

"It is as I said," Turtle's Foot answered. "He expects these Pawnees to have French chiefs."

Villasur glanced at them irritably, and continued.

"When we make contact, I will try to approach them peaceably for a parley. If they prefer a fight, so be it."

There was an answering cheer, which may have left something to be desired in enthusiasm.

"We will sleep until midnight, and then move out," Villasur continued.

He posted watches, and the party separated to seek their all too brief rest before a hard march.

The rising sun found them far downriver, and by mid-morning they were aware of an occasional watcher on a hilltop or across the river. They crossed a stream, one of the biggest tributaries they had encountered so far. It entered the Platte from the north, and presented a landmark that could be used for future reference. Shortly after midday, the scouts, who had withdrawn from their advanced positions, reported a large force on an island in the river not far ahead.

"Ah!" exclaimed Villasur. "This must be the headquarters of the French!"

He called a halt, and asked an orderly for writing materials. Soon he had produced a note, which he folded and sealed with a drop of wax. Then he called for Turtle's Foot and Strong Bow. He spoke to Strong Bow, through the interpreter.

"Now you can be of use. Take this note to your French masters. Here, also, are paper, ink, and quills for an answer."

Strong Bow was completely confused, but now Villasur was continuing, speaking to Turtle's Foot.

"I do not trust him, so you are to go, too, to watch him. This message demands to know their intentions, and I expect a reply."

"We will try, señor," the thoroughly confused interpreter answered. "But what if there are no French?"

Villasur snorted indignantly.

"Of course there are. Do you think me blind? I have seen the looks between the Pawnees and this Strong Bow. I had thought to kill him, but he will be useful for this. Let him carry messages between me and the French command."

There seemed nothing more to be said. The two set out downriver, with many misgivings. They rode openly, to remove all possibility of appearing subversive.

"What do these talking leaves say?" asked Strong Bow, when they were out of earshot.

"I cannot understand the paper's tongue, but the señor said he offers to talk. You are to bring the answer."

"There is much that I do not understand, Turtle."

"I, too."

The main gathering of Pawnees appeared to be on an island in the river. The two scouts stood and studied the situation for a little while.

"It is another town," suggested Turtle's Foot.

"Yes, but there are more men . . . more warriors than there are lodges. This is a gathering, a council."

"Do you see any French?"

Strong Bow looked at his companion and smiled.

"How would we know, my friend? Neither of us has seen any French."

Both chuckled, a little nervously. This could be quite a dangerous situation. Would the French dress in a manner similar to the Spanish, or more like Pawnees?

Strong Bow spoke as he kneed his horse forward. "Well, let us find out!"

Both men rode with right hands raised, palms forward, in the sign of peace. The Pawnees, who had been openly watching them all along, simply stared as the two splashed across the shallow riffle and rode into the village at a walk. They made their way among the staring inhabitants, to a point near the center of the dwellings, and pulled their horses to a stop.

"I would speak with your chief," Strong Bow signed.

There was no answer, only silent stares. Finally, a man emerged from one of the earth-lodges. His dignified bearing marked this one as a leader. He strode boldly forward and stopped face-to-face with the visitors.

"What do you want?" he demanded, in hand-signs.

"We come in peace, Uncle," Strong Bow indicated.

"Then why do your men carry weapons?"

He was not prepared for such a blunt approach, and paused for a moment, caught off balance.

"Ah, Uncle, one does not travel unarmed. But look, I bring a message from our chief."

"What is the message?"

"I do not know, Uncle. It is marked here, on the paper, the talking leaves."

"That means nothing to me!"

This was not going well at all. Strong Bow looked around the circle of stern-faced warriors who surrounded them. None looked the least bit sympathetic. To make matters worse, many of them carried guns, the new thundersticks like those of the Spanish. They must have been obtained in trade with someone, probably French. This thought recalled his primary mission.

"Of course not, my chief. The marks mean nothing to us, either. Our chief sends the message to any French who may be here."

"There are no French here," the Pawnee signed angrily.

He strode forward, chin jutting in a challenging attitude.

"You will tell me what you really want here!"

Strong Bow was perplexed. Twice in recent days, someone had refused to believe him when he spoke the truth. He was not accustomed to such treatment.

"My chief," he signed firmly. "We have spoken truth. If there are French, it is good. I will give you this packet for them. See, the message, and more paper and the feather to mark with, so that I may take back an answer. But you say there *are* no French. That, too, is good. I will tell our leader."

He reined his horse aside, handing the packet as he did so.

The Pawnee pushed it aside.

"No! You will not go back!"

"My chief, your people and mine have no quarrel with each other. Take the message and do with it what you wish. I will tell the Spanish."

"No," signed the other. "You will stay here."

Strong Bow glanced quickly around the area for a path of escape. There was none. In every direction were armed men, determined-looking warriors who appeared intent on preventing any escape.

How stupid, Strong Bow now realized, *to ride into such a situation.* He had not been prepared for this. In his experience, the visit of any stranger under the peace sign had always been honored. His own people, their Head Splitter allies, the Growers, and the people of his pueblo relatives, all honored the approach of a peaceful traveler. Why were these Horn People different? Could it be that there actually *were* French in the area, stirring up enmity with the Spanish? He had the strong impression that this was not a personal thing, or a quarrel with the People as a whole. What, then?

His heart beat faster, and he tried to retain a calm and dignified appearance.

"I am saddened, my chief, by your distrust. I have approached you with good in my heart, but I . . ."

This attempt to smooth over the crisis was interrupted by a sudden move on the part of Turtle's Foot. He had been growing increasingly restless. Now, apparently unable to tolerate the growing threat, Turtle made a desperate effort to escape. With a yell, he kicked his horse forward, directly into the ranks of warriors who circled them.

The first leap of the frightened animal knocked several men sprawling. Its hooves pounded over flesh and bone as others jumped aside to avoid the charge. Someone grabbed at the bridle rein, and the horse reared high, standing on its hind legs, striking out with its forefeet. The man who had grabbed the bridle went down, and Turtle's Foot pulled his horse free and plunged on.

A broad path had opened as men jumped to safety. The horse surged to a lope and threaded into the opening. One, two, three long leaps . . . In another moment he would reach safety, at least for the moment, behind the shelter of the earth-lodges. An arrow flew harmlessly past his head, then another. For a moment it appeared that the bold escape attempt would succeed. Then a musket cracked. The fugitive threw up both arms and fell backward, somersaulting from his mount to strike the ground heavily. He did not move as the riderless horse pounded on. There was a flash of knives and axes as men swarmed over the prostrate figure.

Strong Bow sat still. He had been caught completely off guard by the ill-fated move. He might have joined the attempt, but it was too late now. Someone grabbed his horse's rein, effectively preventing any move. Hands dragged him from the horse, and he fell heavily, knocking the breath from his lungs. As he lay gasping to regain it, he saw a warrior raise an ax for the death blow. He was unable to move, even to defend himself.

Then a strong hand gripped the ax-wielder's wrist. There was a brief argument, and the warrior relaxed. As Strong Bow regained his breath, he saw that the Pawnee chief had intervened in his behalf, at least temporarily.

Rough hands rolled him over and tied his wrists, jerking the thongs cruelly tight behind him. In the distance, he could hear the loose horse that had been the mount of Turtle's Foot, clattering and splashing across the stream in its flight.

The excitement began to calm. He was almost face down in the dust of the town, but out of the corner of his eye he could see fluttering papers . . . the talking leaves, intended for French eyes that might not even exist.

13
›› ›› ››

Strong Bow lay where they had shoved him, aside from the activity of the village. It was dark now, but fires lighted the area, and it was apparent that there was something going on, something of great importance. He had the impression that more warriors were arriving constantly. It seemed that some sort of council was in progress. With the arrival of each new group, each one or two, even, there was renewed excitement. Dance drums and songs kept a constant rhythm, rising and falling as excitement mounted.

He shifted his position, trying to ease the discomfort of his bound wrists. They had tied his feet, too, but there was not as much pain there. His feet were numb, like his hands, but the thongs seemed not to cut so deeply. Maybe it was because his hands were tied behind him, in an awkward position that allowed him to lie only on his side or on his face.

He tried to assess his situation as logically as he could. It was not good. They would probably kill him, and he hoped that he would be able to show them how a man of the People could die. Proudly, showing no fear. He wondered what tortures might precede the event.

Turtle's Foot was dead. He had no doubt of that. He had seen men waving articles stripped from Turtle's body: his knife, bow and quiver, even a necklace. He also thought he saw a bloody scalp. He wondered why they had not killed him, too. He could think of only one reason: Turtle had tried a bold escape, while Strong Bow himself had been still negotiating. He would have tried more negotiation, but could not do so with his hands tied. He had no knowledge of the Pawnee tongue at all, nor they of his, apparently.

He watched the warriors as excitement mounted. Three newcomers drifted into the circle of firelight, and were greeted by those already there. He thought he recognized one of the new arrivals. Was this man not present at the story fire? It seemed long ago now, when they had camped with the Pawnees at the first town they encountered. He wished he could go back and live the last few days over again. *Aiee,* he would not be lying here now, helplessly trussed!

Strong Bow watched the man who had caught his attention. There was something familiar about him . . . the way he carried his head, the shape of his ears, maybe. No, he finally decided. It was impossible to tell. All Horn People looked alike, anyway. But he continued to wonder. It *was* possible that this was a major gathering, a meeting like the Big Council of his own people. If so, it could be for the purpose of planning an attack on the Spanish exploring party. Maybe Villasur, suspicious as he was, could be right. Maybe the French *were* inciting the Pawnees to attack. Strong Bow had seen no one who appeared French. But, he reminded himself, he would not know what a Frenchman looked like.

He sighed and changed his position again. His hands

were numb and wooden, his leg muscles cramped from
inactivity. He turned his head and tried to estimate how
much of the night had passed. There was the Real-star,
through the opening in the trees. And yes, the Seven
Hunters, making their nightly circle around their lodge
at the star. *Aiee,* the night was young yet. It would be a
long time until morning. He had begun to think that
whatever they might do to him would probably begin
with the dawn of day. He dreaded it, but was beginning
to be impatient. Whatever was to be done to him, let it
begin.

He was completely surprised, then, at a sudden
change in the mood of the gathering. A warrior came in,
and the crowd quieted to listen to him. The songs and
the drums stopped. Strong Bow could not understand
the words, but it was clear that this was a scout, a "wolf,"
reporting what he had observed. There were a few questions from those who appeared to be the chiefs, and then
a roar of approval. There was a concerted movement out
of the camp. Not a rush, but a deliberate evacuation. He
could hear the muffled sound of the hundreds of moccasined feet as they splashed across the riffle and onto
the north bank.

Then it was quiet. If anything, the quiet was worse
than the drums and chanting. It made him even more
anxious. There were a few people moving about, old
people and women. The women were collected in small
groups, discussing the events that were occurring. There
was a quiet, sinister mood. It was apparent that the men
of the village, as well as all the visitors from other clans,
had gone on a specific mission. That could be only one: to
attack the Spanish camp. Probably at daylight, he decided. He did not know whether Pawnees fought in the
dark. The People did, but some tribes . . . well, the
Head Splitters, their allies, avoided a night fight at all
costs. In case of death, a spirit leaving the body, it was

thought, would become lost. It would wander forever in darkness, never able to cross over to the Other Side. He had had no occasion to learn whether Pawnees also feared this crossing-over in darkness. However, dawn was a good time to attack, anyway. The growing light, the sleep-weakened condition of the adversary . . .

He wondered where Villasur and his party had camped. They had expected a message, returned by Strong Bow and Turtle's Foot, and would have none. There was no way to guess what Villasur might choose to do. He would be attacked; the only question was, where?

Strong Bow's bladder was becoming uncomfortably full. He hated to give in to the discomfort and soil himself, and wondered how long he could wait before relief was necessary. He was also becoming very thirsty. That was uncomfortable, but he could stand it. Maybe someone would notice the prisoner and see to his needs, but probably not. Even that would be a mixed blessing. He tried not to think about the fact that among tribes who torture, the women were said to enjoy the process the most. There were gruesome tales of the skillful use of knives on tender parts . . . *Aiee,* he must try not to think of such things!

It was nearly morning when someone first noticed the prisoner. A young woman . . . that might be good or bad, he thought. A young woman might have motherly instincts and feel sorry for him. It was equally possible that a woman this age could have a sadistic streak that would be too horrible to think of.

The girl was passing by, possibly going outside the area to relieve her own bladder. She glanced aside at the huddled form beside the mounded earth-lodge, and stepped over to investigate. There was only a little light from the dying fire, and she stood and studied the situation for a moment. Then she spoke, in her own tongue, a few words that could have meant anything, but meant nothing to the prisoner. He shook his head to indicate that he did not understand. The young woman nodded, and began to use hand-signs.

"You are the prisoner."

Her attitude was neutral, neither hostile nor friendly. Maybe he could keep her attention, keep her interested long enough to make her see him as a person, not merely a captive nonentity.

He shrugged and moved his bound hands so that she could see them better. His status was obvious, and the girl perceived the uselessness of her question. She gave a little half-smile, almost apologetically, barely discernible in the dim firelight.

"What are you doing here?" she now signed.

Instantly, she realized how ridiculous the question was. He could not use hand-signs, and did not know her tongue.

She gave a short little laugh.

"I am sorry. You cannot answer."

He nodded, smiling ruefully. He tried to think of any words of Pawnee that he might know, but could remember none.

"I am sorry, too," he said in his own tongue, knowing that she could not understand. He tried to make the tone pleasant, his general attitude friendly. "I wish that I *could* talk to you," he went on. "It would help if my hands were untied."

She nodded, her face friendly but her expression showing plainly that she understood nothing he said. She was pretty, at least moderately so. It was hard to tell in the semidark, and with her face still smeared with the red face-paint that the Pawnee women used so freely. Her body was slim and shapely. She was probably not married, he decided. If she had a husband, she would not be talking to a strange man, especially a prisoner. Except, maybe, to revile him or torture him.

He licked his dry, parched lips, an involuntary move, but the girl noticed it instantly.

"Water?" she signed.

He nodded.

"I will bring it."

She glided away, and soon returned with a gourd. There seemed to be a little hesitancy about approaching him, but she seemed to realize that he was helpless, and therefore harmless. She dropped to her knees, and held the gourd to his lips.

The water was warm, and tasted a little muddy, but it was wet and wonderful. She let him drink, three times, and then sat back on her heels, setting the gourd bottle aside. He nodded his thanks.

"I am made to think," she signed, "that you are not an enemy."

Strong Bow shook his head vigorously, and the girl laughed.

"As an enemy would say," she chided. But her expression was friendly now.

His bladder discomfort was still increasing, and he wondered if she could help him. He hated to call attention to his unprotected genitals, but to wet himself certainly would do so, and in an unpleasant way. She was friendly enough. There would surely be no threat of knives and torture from this one. He nodded his head toward his groin, and glanced in that direction, a pained expression on his face.

She seemed puzzled for a moment, then began to sign.

"What? Your bladder?"

Strong Bow nodded vigorously.

The girl seemed to consider for a little while.

"How . . . ?" she started to sign, and then shook her head. "No!" she signed firmly. "You will have to wait until morning. I will help you if I can."

She jumped to her feet, picked up the gourd, and was gone, flitting gracefully into the darkness.

Strong Bow lay there, helpless, still in agony from his bladder, but he felt more optimistic now. He *could* relieve himself if necessary. He would try to control it a little longer. Mostly, however, his optimism was because of the girl. Maybe she could do nothing to help him, but she had promised to try. It was a better feeling than his thoughts about torture.

He thought of the hundred or so of Villasur's party, camped somewhere out there in the darkness. Dawn would be critical for them, too. He hoped they would be alert, but from what he had seen, it would not matter much. Even readiness against surprise would not help much if they were outnumbered as badly as he suspected. Even so, he had still seen no evidence of French, or "Huguenots" as Villasur called them.

There was still much that Strong Bow did not understand, but one thing was plain. Villasur and the others had not a single friend among the Pawnees. Strong Bow, at least, had one.

14

>> >> >>

Villasur peered into the darkness. There were sounds out there, sounds of the night. The call of an owl, the croak of a frog, the cry of a coyote on a distant hill. There were also the sounds that the sentries had reported several times during the night. Splashing sounds, as if, for example, large numbers of men were crossing the river. They had tried to investigate, but found nothing. Probably beavers or perhaps otters at play, he decided.

He was disgruntled that his plan to contact the French and negotiate had failed. He was not sure why. They had waited for a while, expecting the return of one or both of the messengers, hopefully with a letter from the French commander. He would negotiate, once he knew their intentions.

But his answer never came. Probably, he decided, it was a mistake to send those he suspected were traitors. They had simply joined the Pawnees and their French masters, and had no intention of returning.

He had been concerned by the single musket shot in

the distance. It had not been fired by one of his soldiers. Therefore, since there were no other Spanish troops in the area, the weapon that fired the shot must have been French. Whether it had been held by a native or by one of their French officers was of minor importance. He did wonder about the circumstances. It would seem that from the viewpoint of the French, it would be best to avoid detection. That, of course, would be the explanation for the fact that his party had seen no French.

Was the distant shot an accidental discharge, then? Or . . . perhaps his emissaries, or at least the pueblo interpreter . . . Of course! That was it! Strong Bow was in league with the Pawnees and French. When he arrived with the unfortunate interpreter, Turtle's Foot must have been killed to remove him.

Villasur had been certain that whatever action the enemy intended was near at hand. The day was nearly spent, and his troops were in a poor tactical position. He called a retreat. It was an orderly withdrawal, of course, with the exception of the undisciplined natives, who milled about excitedly. They did not understand military tactics.

His plan was to draw back to the junction of the rivers. The point of land where the two streams met seemed ideal for defensive positions. Attackers would have to cross rivers on both north and south sides of the long wedge of land that separated the streams. Therefore, the defense could be concentrated across the third side of the triangle, the land approach from the west. He had a strong sense of satisfaction for having deduced this plan. He could already envision his report to the Governor, with maps and sketches of troop movements.

They had reached the junction and the last of the Spanish party had crossed the river to the selected area just before dark. They had posted heavy guard, and the sentries assumed their stations. The word was passed:

There would be no fires. Grumbling, most of the tired troops sought their blankets, but for Villasur there would be no sleep. There was too much excitement in the air.

Now it was nearly morning. He had spent the long night peering into the dark, listening to nature's night-sounds. When would the attack come, he wondered. The French would undoubtedly march their forces around to the north, cross the smaller river some distance up-stream, and launch a frontal attack by land. All of that would take time. He did not believe that the maneuvering could be accomplished before noon, so that was the likeliest time for the strike.

He was wrong, horribly wrong. He watched the yellow-gray of the false dawn begin to lighten the sky in the east. Night-sounds became less frequent, replaced by the sleepy chirps and twitters of birds coming awake and beginning to move about. Stars were fading, and he saw the silent form of a great owl glide silently across the lightening sky.

Precisely at dawn, the attack came. There was a shot, then another, then a ragged volley. The air seemed full of buzzing things, like angry bees. With a sense of wonder, he realized that these were musket balls. Horned warriors were everywhere, their war cries mingling with the screams of the wounded.

Villasur himself was one of the first to fall. The Pawnee seemed to rise out of the earth before his eyes, raising the musket as he did so. He watched, horrified but not quite understanding. There was an unreality about it in the misty gray of dawn, as if this were happening to someone else. How large the round muzzle looked as it swung toward him and steadied for an instant. Then the hammer fell, and the pan flashed. An instant later the mouth of the weapon belched orange fire. The heavy lead ball smashed into his body, throwing him to the ground. Half conscious, he watched a spreading red stain darkening his rust-colored tunic. He saw men running, falling, but the scene seemed to have no meaning.

One of the priests ran past, fleeing for his life, a blanket around his head and shoulders.

"Father!" Villasur called weakly. "Bless me, for I . . ."

The priest hesitated, started to turn, and then was struck down from behind with an ax by a horned warrior. He was dead almost instantly, but hardly before the blanket was ripped from his head. The warrior reached to take the scalp, and grunted in disappointment, staring for a moment at the shaved pate. Then he laughed at the joke on himself, and moved on.

Villasur's perception of what was occurring was fading rapidly as his lifeblood ebbed. One of his last thoughts was a puzzled one: *But where are the French?*

The ragged remnants of Villasur's expedition were retreating now, running west along the Platte. The pueblo people had realized the hopelessness of the situation first, so their casualties were lighter. Scarcely a dozen Spaniards were left alive to carry the tale of the tragic debacle back to Governor Valverde in Santa Fe. Don Pedro de Villasur's mission was over.

Some distance to the east, Strong Bow still lay tied hand and foot. It was now daylight, and people were beginning to stir. Women built cooking fires and moved about with the morning chores of fuel and water. There was, of course, an air of anticipation. The men were absent, except for the very young and the very old.

Long rays of new sunlight made horizontal lines of gold through the trees. Under other circumstances it might have been a pleasant morning, but for Strong Bow it was probably the worst of his life. His hands were swollen, chafed, and bloody from the rawhide thongs. The exposed skin areas of his body were now welted with the bites of mosquitoes. Perhaps worst of all was his full bladder. He had not yet been willing to discard his dignity.

An old man shuffled past, glancing curiously at the prisoner as he passed. Probably, thought Strong Bow, he was going out to urinate. Even this tottering oldster could avail himself of what now seemed the greatest of luxuries.

"Ah-koh!" he called to the man.

The old man paused, then shuffled nearer. Strong Bow motioned with his head, encouraging the approach.

"Uncle," he said, "I know that you cannot understand my words, but I need help, here."

The man stopped, studying the prisoner. Surely, thought Strong Bow, he could find some way to communicate his plight. The old man's own bladder should tell him something. He tried to motion toward his own groin with motions of his head, but the old man seemed not to understand. He made no answer at all, and finally turned to shuffle away, muttering to himself.

It seemed a long time later that the two women approached. One was the girl who had visited him in the night. She was pretty, even in the more revealing light of day. The other was an older woman, who could be the mother. Yes, that was logical. The girl was probably still living in her mother's lodge.

The expression on the face of the older woman was far from reassuring. It was a glowering, unforgiving scowl that sent chills through his already chilled body. He tried to convince himself that the girl wished to help him, and would not bring harm down on him. This assurance was not entirely successful. He now saw that the older woman carried a small ax, held loosely in her right hand. This he perceived as an ominous sign at first. His thoughts told him that it did not concern him. If they were preparing to kill him, it would not be quickly, with an ax. It would be by slow torture. That, in turn, was not a pleasant thought, but at least seemed to postpone the inevitable. Surely, nothing would be done with a prisoner, anyway, until the return of the men. He wondered how long that would be.

Meanwhile, the two women were engaged in discussion. Finally they seemed to come to an agreement. The girl began to sign.

"We will loose your hands and retie them in front," she informed him. "My mother will kill you if you try to run."

As if in emphasis, the other woman raised her ax slightly, and then let it fall back to her side. He had been right, then. This was the girl's mother.

The older woman worked at the thongs for a moment, muttered under her breath, and then slashed the rawhide with her knife. Strong Bow could hardly lift his arms, but attempted to rub a little circulation back into his hands. He hardly recognized them. Fat and swollen, they looked more like the paws of a bear. Gingerly, he worked his fingers a little.

"It is good," he signed. "I give my thanks!"

"Hurry up!" the older woman ordered. "We must retie you again."

"Of course! But how? I cannot walk or even stand!"

There was a pause, and a little discussion between the women.

"How could I hurt anyone with these bear paws?" he asked, holding up his swollen hands.

"You could run!" accused the woman.

Strong Bow doubted that. He would hardly be able to stand or bear weight on his feet immediately.

The woman spoke to her daughter and then turned to sign again. "We will retie your feet."

The girl knelt and tied another thong from one ankle to the other, leaving enough slack for a short step only.

Then she freed the tight bonds and stepped back. The mother stood, ax ready for any treachery.

"Get up!" she demanded.

Painfully, Strong Bow struggled to his feet. A thousand tiny thorns seemed to jab into his feet and ankles as the circulation returned. He nearly fell, but steadied himself.

"Go on!" gestured the ax-woman.

"This way?" Strong Bow gestured, taking a tentative step or two. He took the direction he had seen the old man use previously. The two women followed.

His steps were not only painful, but uncomfortably short, because of the hobble on his ankles. He finally reached an area away from the lodges, and stopped, turning to ask.

"Go ahead," the woman signed impatiently.

He loosened his breechclout. Even with the two women watching, this was the most marvelous sensation he had ever experienced, the release of pressure from his overextended bladder. His stream seemed to go on and on. He could feel his belly become flatter and more comfortable. Even the women seemed astonished at the vast capacity of his bladder. Finally the stream dwindled and ceased. He turned with a smile of relief.

"Back!" the woman gestured toward the lodges.

"Of course, Mother," he signed, feeling almost jovial. He shuffled back the way they had come.

When they reached the area they had left, he stopped, and turned, questioning.

"Here?"

"Yes . . . No, over here!"

They led him to a small tree, and the older woman gestured for him to place his arms around it. He was reluctant.

"Must I be tied?" he questioned. He extended his swollen hands again. "How could I do harm with these?"

She hefted her ax menacingly. "Look, Bear Paws, I will tie you tighter than before . . ."

Hastily, he thrust his hands around the small trunk so that she could tie him again. He glanced aside at the younger woman, and was pleased to see a look of sympathy on her face. It was not much to go on, but better than nothing.

The woman finished her task, and turned to stride away. The girl lingered a moment, and the mother called back over her shoulder an obvious command to "come on."

Hastily, the girl, looking somewhat mischievous, signed to him.

"I will come back, Bear Paws." He tried to relax, and of course it was impossible. He was more comfortable, though. They had selected an area of shade, and had tied him with more consideration than before. His future certainly looked no worse, and possibly better, than he had thought earlier. This mother and daughter actually seemed concerned for his welfare. They had given him a name . . . "Bear Paws." He chuckled ruefully. At least it was better than "Full Bladder."

But what would happen when the men returned?

15

>> >> >>

It was mid-morning when the first of the returning warriors arrived. They could be heard before that, excitedly singing, laughing, and calling out to each other.

The very first emissary splashed across the riffle, entered the village, and vaulted from his horse with a shout of victory. People began to gather. Before the news of the great victory was hardly announced, more warriors began to straggle in, by ones and twos, sometimes singly. A few were mounted, most were on foot. There were a few casualties, mostly minor injuries. One series of wails suggested that at least one family had lost a warrior, and was singing the Pawnee equivalent of the People's Song of Mourning.

It was not reassuring. Strong Bow sat watching the returnees, less uncomfortable than he had been, but at least as apprehensive. His hands were tied.

No sooner had that thought crossed his mind than his worst fears were realized. A woman rushed toward him. It was one whom he had just noticed participating in the

Mourning Song, and her eyes flashed hatred as she trotted across the clearing toward him. She was screaming at
him, words he did not understand, and she carried a
skinning knife. From her apparent age, he guessed that
perhaps a son, or maybe her husband, had been one of
the casualties. There was little time to think of that. He
was completely helpless, unable to defend himself.

"I did not kill him!" he yelled at her. Even as he did so,
he knew that she could not understand him.

The woman stopped directly in front of him. Her red
face-paint made her appearance all the more threatening. She showed him the knife, and smiled. It was not a
friendly smile. Her eyes glittered grimly. She toyed with
the knife, running her glance over his helpless body. Her
gaze lingered suggestively on his breechclout, and the
muscles of his groin tightened.

So this is how it begins, he thought. He must bear up
under the torture, and die with dignity, befitting a man
of the People. It would not be an easy death. He wondered if it would be possible to allow the spirit to cross
over early in the procedure, relieving one's body of the
uselessness of pain. For all practical purposes, he was
already dead. But he wondered. Would that be an escape? Was it proper to think of avoiding the pain of the
torture by causing early death? The object was to stay
alive and show with stoic resolve how well a man of the
People could *bear* pain. But the woman turned on her
heel and stalked away, wailing again.

Having decided what he was expected to do, he now
wondered if he *could* behave with dignity. It would
probably be amusing to his torturers if he lost his resolve
and screamed, or even moaned.

What form would it take? He was very uncomfortable
over the way the knife-woman was eyeing his private
parts. Surely it would not begin with that. First, maybe,
strips of skin from his chest, back, or belly. An ear, fingers

. . . He was not certain why it made a difference. There was no possibility of survival anyway. Which of his parts first separated from the rest was of little long-range importance. Still, it was hard to comprehend that when Sun Boy greeted the world tomorrow, there would be no Strong Bow.

That was another thing . . . his name. When he did not return, his family would sooner or later realize that he was dead. Among the People, it was forbidden to speak the name of the dead. That was the reason for one of their traditional customs, that of giving away one's name. If someone else wears it, there is no taboo. However, was there any other Strong Bow? He had never given his name. There had been no occasion to do so, and he had intended to use it for a long time.

A similar situation had occurred before, he now recalled. A popular young leader, whose name was . . . Red Hawk, or something of the sort. The man had been killed during a great buffalo hunt, while still too young to have given away his name, the story said. It so happened that there was no other in all the bands named Red Hawk, so both words were lost from the language. No one could speak Red or Hawk forever. It had been necessary to create new words for those things.

Now, Strong Bow wondered, would there be new words for Strong and Bow? He could think of no other . . . Ah! Was there not a boy in the Northern band? No, that was *Short* Bow. Well, it would be of little concern to Strong Bow.

He shifted his position and looked at his hands. They still looked fat, but not quite so much so. He could partly close the left one now. Gingerly, he rubbed his chafed wrists, trying to massage the swelling back into circulation.

No one seemed to be paying much attention to him. Everyone was too busy celebrating the great victory, or mourning their loved ones. There seemed to be very little mourning, however. Apparently the Pawnee losses had been light.

He saw wet and bloody scalps, waved aloft by singing warriors. Some were wearing Spanish tunics or other parts of Spanish uniforms. Weapons, too. He recognized the pattern of a musket as slightly different from the French style that his captors had had before. One warrior brandished a "long knife," the saber that had been worn by Villasur. *He will not need it,* thought Strong Bow. He was just beginning to realize how complete the defeat had been.

A warrior trotted into the open area, and motioned for others to join him. Strong Bow saw that he carried something in a sack that may have been formed from an article of wearing apparel. The warrior loosened his bundle and rolled the contents out on the ground . . . a human head! In another instant, Strong Bow recognized the shaven head of the Spanish holy man. The warrior was explaining, telling the story of his kill, and everyone was laughing. Strong Bow was puzzled, but then realized that the man was relating his attempt to scalp the bald pate, and the frustration that resulted. It had been considered such a joke that he had brought the whole head to assist in the telling and retelling of his tale.

He finished, shrugged with an exaggerated, puzzled expression, and the crowd roared with laughter.

Then his eye fell on the prisoner, and he trotted over, drawing his scalping knife. His intention was plain. He had been cheated out of one scalp, but here was an easy replacement. Strong Bow's skin crawled as the hand reached to grab his hair. People were sometimes scalped alive . . . Strong Bow had not even thought of that. The first slash could have been in a worse area, but . . .

The knife-woman now shouldered forward, loudly protesting. Strong Bow realized that they were arguing over whose privilege it would be to cut the prisoner. Now the warrior backed down before the woman's tirade. His attitude was placating, apologetic. The onlookers were enjoying all of this immensely. This man must be a well-known jokester, Strong Bow guessed. There had been no serious intention to scalp the prisoner. The whole thing was a joke, a bitter joke. He also suspected that it was no joke for the woman. Her intentions, whatever they were, were much more to be feared than those of the jokester.

As if to reassure the prisoner of her intent, she paused before him for a moment.

"You are mine!" she signed, very seriously.

The crowd laughed again as the woman turned away. In the crowd, Strong Bow saw the face of the girl who had helped him. Her face was tense and serious. Would she be able to help him again?

An ugly thought came to him. Was his torture being postponed for a reason? A special celebration, perhaps, after the excitement of victory was diminished? A treat that no one would want to miss, the torture and death of this captive? His was a strange mixture of fear and anger, at the realization that he was to be the guest of honor in this spectacle. He had seen no other prisoners, so he must be the only object of torture. Every technique of torture would be reserved for him alone, while the crowd laughed and jeered at every slash, every flinch. And if this coming event did occur as he feared, the object of the game would be to see how long he could be kept alive without losing consciousness. The whole thing would be a bigger joke than the bald head of the Spanish holy man.

About midday, the pretty girl and her mother returned. They brought him water and a few bites of tough, poorly cooked meat. Probably scraps that would have been fed to the dogs otherwise, he decided, but he was grateful for any consideration. They untied his hands long enough for him to feed himself, but when he began to sign, the mother motioned with her ax, and he was quickly tied again.

In his own mind, he was thinking of this one as Ax-Woman, and the threatening one who was in mourning as Knife-Woman. The girl, of course, was Pretty One.

He wished that afternoon that he had not thought of the scraps of meat as dog scraps. That led him to think of the way a woman makes a pet of a dog that is being fattened for slaughter. In order to catch it more easily, she feeds it small morsels often. Then it comes near without suspicion, and does not even try to dodge the club that ends its life.

Were these two treating him with a little kindness so that he would be more manageable? Maybe . . . He almost envied the dog, whose end would come instantly when the day arrived that it became food for the family. Strong Bow's end would not be swift, but long and painful. He tried to put that out of his mind.

Through the afternoon the rejoicing and singing continued, in celebration of victory. Toward evening he noticed that people were bringing fuel, large quantities of wood for some sort of event. He hesitated to think of *what* sort of event. He had been so intent on the damage that could be done with knives and skewers that he had overlooked one possibility: Some tribes roasted prisoners, he had heard.

He had no objection to such a practice . . . It was, after all, *their* custom, not that of the People. He did resent being the object of such a roast. Especially if he happened to be still alive. He thought again of the dog, now with envy.

It was nearly dark, and the great council fire had been lighted, when Ax-Woman and Pretty One returned. He was given water, and allowed to empty his bladder again. But instead of returning him to his tree, they pointed toward the council fire.

It appeared that everyone in the village was present, as well as extra warriors. He was sure that he recognized men from the village far to the west, where they had spent the night and exchanged stories. *Aiee,* how long ago that seemed now. And how different the circumstances!

16
>> >> >>

Lone Elk had some concerns about the celebration. It had indeed been a great victory, one of the greatest in the history of his clan. He was pleased that his had been the area chosen by the council to attack the Spaniards.

Shortly after the Morning Star ceremony that summer, the word had come. A party of hairfaces from the southwest, more than a hundred, it was said, was advancing across the plains. It was said that they were asking of the French, but there had been no French for several seasons. A generation ago, yes. They had traded some with the newcomers, for metal knives, tools, and a few guns. There had been little trouble. The French liked Pawnee women, and the strangeness of the newcomers' customs was, in turn, exciting to the women.

One thing the French did not seem to understand, though. The choice belonged to the women. Eventually, there came to be bad feelings between the two groups. One too many of the voyageurs tried to force his attentions on an unwilling woman. The woman had been

stabbed, as he remembered the story . . . It had happened at another village. That led to ill feelings, and the
French withdrew from the whole area.

It was too bad, Lone Elk thought. They had lost that
source of metal. It was also hard to get powder and balls
for the muskets. Some of the traveling Arapaho, the
"Trading People," would sometimes supply small quantities, but at great price in trade.

This new situation had seemed ideal. An armed party,
carrying muskets, powder, lead, and supplies! They
could stop the threat, and at the same time acquire the
supplies and more muskets.

It was too bad about the young man of the Elk-dog
People who had been with the Spanish. He had seemed
honest enough. He was of a tribe known to Lone Elk, one
which hunted and lived on the plains to the south. They
seldom traded with the Pawnees, because they could
trade with other grower tribes closer to their own territory. So, this young man's people, while not allies, were
not enemies, either. Probably his statement was true. He
had been employed as an interpreter, nothing more,
nothing less. He used hand-signs well, as would be expected of a young man of the Elk-dog People.

Lone Elk had listened to the reports of the Spanish
party's stopover at one of the villages to the west. This
same young man, Strong Bow, he called himself, had
made a good impression with his stories. That village's
old storyteller, who knew the Elk-dog People, had reported that the young man had known his stories and
told them well. That was added reason to accept Strong
Bow for what he claimed to be.

There had been an added near-incident, it seemed.
Both the Spanish and the natives who accompanied
them had refused to participate in the story fire. The
Elk-dog man had seemed surprised, had appeared to

understand the rudeness, and had tried to remedy the insult with his own stories. That was good.

When he had appeared as a messenger, carrying the talking leaves, Lone Elk had seen him for the first time, and had been ready to talk. But such things go wrong, sometimes. If the other messenger had not acted so stupidly . . . Ah, well, it was done now. Lone Elk had saved the stranger on an impulse. In light of events since that, it would have been better to let him be killed.

Now there was an argument over what should be done with the prisoner. "Bear Paws," he was being called now, from his swollen hands. Pumpkin Rings, who had lost both a son and her husband in the battle, was demanding the right to publicly torture and kill the prisoner. Her claim was valid, of course, and there was much public sentiment in her favor. This opinion was probably weighted by a desire to watch the torture. There had been little opportunity for such entertainment for several seasons now.

But then Laughing Crow had entered the situation. Ah, that one! Crow could always be counted upon to liven any situation with his jokes, and it must be admitted that this was a good one. To bring the shaved head of a fallen enemy, because there was no scalp . . . Lone Elk chuckled again at the thought. Normally, with no other claims on the prisoner, it would have been amusing to honor Crow's ridiculous claim. This time, the claim only complicated the decision. Laughing Crow's jokes were useful, sometimes, Elk thought. His humor could lighten a grim situation. But this time, Crow showed no sign that he was ready to abandon the joke. Maybe he really expected to harvest the scalp.

Lone Elk considered having a private talk with the jokester to dissuade him. That would be politically desirable, except for the unpredictability of Crow. Suppose Crow refused, and made a public furor over having been asked to give up his demand for the scalp? That would harm Lone Elk's credibility, and diminish his influence as a leader. No, however the dilemma was resolved, it must be openly done.

The more so because of the interference of Elk's own daughter, Pretty Sky. The girl was of marriageable age, but had not yet accepted any of the young men. It was not for lack of opportunity. She was a most desirable woman. There was nothing wrong with Sky's sexual inclinations, her mother reported. She was merely opinionated. Elk had long been aware of *that*, of course.

And now . . . Pretty Sky had assumed that the captive was her father's prisoner. She had seen him stop the ax that would have dealt the death blow.

Why she had been attracted to this Bear Paws he could not understand. It certainly presented a complication. If he gave the prisoner to Pretty Sky, he might appear to be guilty of favoritism. That would not be politically expedient, either.

Ah, sometimes the weight of leadership lay heavily on the shoulders of the chieftain! He had been fortunate to postpone the decision this far only because of the excitement over the victory. At least half the intruders had been killed, and the rest were in full retreat. Some had favored pursuit, but after a short while, cooler heads prevailed. It was foolish to pursue a large group. Sooner or later, someone would turn and fight out of desperation, as a trapped animal will do. That would be dangerous, possibly turning victory songs into songs of mourning. But the entire day's excitement had distracted the thoughts of the villagers from the prisoner. Oh, a few of the young women had stepped over to spit in his face, but there was no urgency in it. No, Elk knew the clan of which he was the leader. They would not push the decision, but would expect it at the festivities tonight. But *how* to resolve this, without favoritism?

For perhaps the hundredth time today he wished that he had let the ax fall. If the prisoner had died, there would have been no problem. Maybe he could . . . No, it would show weakness to take the easy way, to kill the man himself now. Besides, he was forced to admit, he rather liked this prisoner. He could not have said why, but here was a man on the verge of death by torture. Really creative torture, if he judged old Pumpkin Rings correctly. Yet the young man was handling himself well under the circumstances. He still looked proud and dignified, even with his swollen paws. Yes, a proud man who in dying would represent his people well. It was too bad to kill such a man. Maybe . . .

His thoughts were interrupted by the approach of one of the younger warriors.

"Greetings, my chief," said Red Hand. "May I ask something?"

Lone Elk now remembered. It was Red Hand who had held the ax . . .

He nodded. "What is it?"

"My chief, you stopped me from killing this prisoner. Will he be returned to me? Will I be the one who kills him in the celebration tonight?"

Ah, thought Lone Elk, *another one!* He sighed deeply.

"We will see," he told the young man. "What will be will be."

Obviously disappointed, Red Hand nodded. "It is good, my chief," he said, though his attitude belied it.

"You already counted honors on his head, no?" Lone Elk asked.

"Yes, but so did several others, also."

That was true. The captive had been struck several times by various people during the brief scuffle.

"Of course, Red Hand. But let us see what happens. You count your honor in the dance tonight."

Lone Elk did not have any ideas yet. If there were only

some way to keep Bear Paws alive for a while. If the prisoner's attitude proved satisfactory, he might make a good fighting man *for* the Pawnee. In all probability, he would never be asked to fight against his own people. It would be possible, even, to excuse a warrior from a fight that was in conflict with his own allegiance. But *how?*

He watched as Pretty Sky and her mother walked across the open space toward the captive. They carried water and a little food. Elk wondered what his wife might think about the whole situation. Maybe he should talk with her about it. He knew what *he* wanted, but . . .

Suddenly, his eyes widened and his jaw dropped. Ah! Why had he not thought of this before? Of course! There was a way to recognize everyone's claim. He was certain that Kills-Three, his wife, would approve his plan. But maybe he would not tell her. Yes, that was it! He would let her be as completely surprised as the rest.

He chuckled to himself.

"Red Hand," he called to the retreating form, "come back a little while."

Puzzled, the young man returned.

"Yes, my chief?"

"Red Hand, you know that others, too, claim the Bear Paws prisoner?"

It was a statement, not a question.

"Yes . . ."

"Well, if anyone asks, it *will* be decided tonight."

"Yes, my chief."

Red Hand was more confused than ever. He turned away again, and Lone Elk chuckled quietly to himself. If his plan worked, it was possible to satisfy everyone, including himself.

17
>> >> >>

The prisoner stood proudly before the crowd, still showing the dignity that had pleased Lone Elk. In his eye was the look of a captured eagle, fettered but not defeated. *Good,* thought Lone Elk. That would help with his plan.

The excitement that had continued through the day had reached an even higher pitch as darkness fell and the fire was lighted. Everyone in the village, as well as a large number of visiting warriors, crowded the council circle to hear and see the proceedings. There had already been several accounts of the battle from various warriors, who relived their triumphs for the assembled listeners.

Now Lone Elk raised his hands for quiet, and the noise of the crowd simmered down to silence. Even the crack of the fire could be heard, and the sound of a night-bird in the trees across the river.

"Now," Lone Elk began, "we will talk of this prisoner."

There was a ripple of approval.

"He looks healthy," observed Lone Elk. "A good fighting man."

There was laughter.

"But he is our prisoner!" called someone.

More laughter.

"He does not understand our tongue," Lone Elk went on, "but would it not be good to have such a man to fight for us?"

There were a couple of derisive hoots from the rear.

"He fought for the enemy!" someone shouted.

"No!" Elk corrected. "He carried a message for them, and made the hand-sign for peace. The man with him was an enemy."

There was now a mutter of discontent. He must move on.

"But no matter . . . There are others with an interest in this prisoner, this Bear Paws." He paused and looked around the circle. "Red Hand, here, stopped from killing him so that we all have more pleasure in watching it later."

Red Hand swelled with pride at the unexpected flattery.

"And Laughing Crow, our friend of the jokes," Lone Elk went on, "is not joking when he claims the scalp!"

An appreciative wave of laughter rolled across the village. The story of Crow's bald trophy was well known.

"He deserves his trophy," suggested Elk, "but our sister who mourns tonight, Pumpkin Rings, there, has her claim, too. You know what she wants!"

There were serious nods of agreement.

"Now, besides all these, my daughter Pretty Sky has asked for his life."

A hushed murmur of astonishment rippled around the circle. Most had not been aware of this complication.

"Now, I am made to think," Lone Elk said thoughtfully, "that all must have what they wish."

The voices of disbelief, of near-ridicule, were quieted by a gesture.

"Now first, Red Hand will kill him. Then Crow takes the scalp."

Red Hand rose with his throwing ax in hand.

"No, wait," called Lone Elk, as a shout of protest came from old Pumpkin Rings. "Then he cannot be tortured. Let him be scalped first, then killed."

"No, I will do the torture!" the old woman cried, shouldering forward. She lifted her knife and pointed it at the stoic-faced prisoner.

"Wait, this must be done right, my friends," Lone Elk protested. "If Pumpkin Rings has her turn first, Bear Paws will be of little use for my daughter's purpose."

The crowd roared with laughter. Lone Elk's meaning was all too apparent.

"I am made to think," Lone Elk went on as if in deep thought, "that the order in which these claims are fulfilled is the important part. Let each take a turn, but that one first who leaves something for the others."

"How is this?" demanded Pumpkin Rings angrily.

"I give him to Pretty Sky first," Lone Elk explained. "She keeps him as a pet dog for a while, then gives him to you. When you say so, Laughing Crow can take his scalp, then finally Red Hand will kill him."

"By that time, he will beg to die," chortled Pumpkin Rings. She pointed her knife at the prisoner and continued her threats in sign talk. "You are mine," she gestured, "one part at a time!"

The crowd laughed, and Lone Elk felt a glow of satisfaction. His plan was working, they were relaxing.

"Wait!" a voice called. "He will escape!"

"No," Elk promised. "Red Hand will see that he does not."

Red Hand nodded enthusiastically. "I will not miss my turn," he promised.

Now Pumpkin Rings thrust her knife under his nose. "See that you do not take someone else's turn," she threatened.

The crowd howled with glee . . . It was as Elk had hoped. They were no longer angry, thirsting for blood.

"Cut his hands loose," he ordered, "so that he can talk."

This was accomplished, and the prisoner rubbed his wrists.

"Bear Paws," Lone Elk signed, "you will live for now. You will do as you are told. If you try to escape, that one will kill you." He pointed to Red Hand. "If you do *not* obey, you will be given to *that* one . . ." He indicated Pumpkin Rings.

The prisoner turned to her. "I am sorry for your loss, Mother. It was not my doing," he signed.

"Liar!" she screamed at him, though he did not understand her word.

She stepped forward, and Lone Elk thought for a moment that he would have to stop her. But there was no weapon in her hand, and he refrained. The woman slapped the prisoner across the face, hard, then spat on him. Spittle trickled down his cheek, and he wiped it away, still maintaining his dignity. She drew back to strike him again, but Lone Elk intervened.

"It is good, woman. But it is enough for now. Your turn will come."

Pumpkin Rings stared for a moment, then touched her knife hilt and nodded significantly. She turned away, beginning again her keening wail of mourning as she threaded her way through the crowd and into the night. All eyes followed her, and Lone Elk took advantage of the moment to sign quickly to the prisoner.

"Be careful of that onc."

Bear Paws nodded.

It was good, thought Lone Elk. The woman had gotten rid of some of her hurt, and the ceremony of mourning would rid her of more. Hopefully, she would forget her intent to inflict the obscenities of torture on Bear Paws.

But now the onlookers were turning back.

"Let us continue the victory dance!" he cried. "I will take the prisoner for now."

There was a wave of approval. He tied Bear Paws to a tree in plain sight of all, judging him to be safe now. Safer, at least, than he would be somewhere in the darkness. Lone Elk was still not quite ready to trust the woman who had vowed vengeance on the person of this man.

It was nearly morning before the festivities slowed to a stop and ceased. Tired dancers straggled off to find their sleeping robes.

Strong Bow had watched the ceremonies with a great deal of vested interest. He was not completely certain what had transpired. It was apparent that there had been an argument over what should be done with him, but it had been resolved. Just how, he did not understand. He was certain of one thing. The greatest threat to his life was the woman with the knife, the one who mourned. The way her eyes glittered when she looked at him . . . *aiee*, it was unnerving!

The man who was apparently the leader of this village had signed to him that his life was to be spared. There was no indication as to how long. There had also been the warning, short and puzzling. A warning that the prisoner had not needed, to remain alert where the knife-woman was concerned. He already feared her.

There was something else in the attitude of the chief. Strong Bow had a definite feeling of good will on the part of this man. There was no question in his mind, the leader of this band of the Horn People wanted to *help* the prisoner. The reason for this was unclear.

After the council and the decision, whatever it had been, he had been tied in a prominent place. For a while he was afraid that he had misunderstood the evening's events, that they were preparing to torture or burn him alive. But there were no overt actions to cause concern. From time to time, someone would come over to sneer and taunt him, perhaps even spit on him or slap him. These acts, however, seemed to be important only in themselves, not a prelude to anything worse. He felt that he was placed on display, like the trophies of the victory that were paraded proudly around the village.

Yes, that must be it, he thought. There was no intensity, no increasing in violence as the night progressed. He saw this as a good sign. Then, too, the longer he remained alive, the better for him. If they began to think of the prisoner as a person, rather than merely a symbol of their enemies, that should help. It was a thing in his favor that they had given him a name: Bear Paws. He must accept this, for now.

He tried to maintain the dignity that was so important. That was not easy, for he was very tired. He felt like slumping against the tree to which he was tied. That would have been a comfort, of sorts, but would have shown weakness. So, he stood erect, trying to keep his facial expression calm and dignified, and to show no fear.

A group of small children approached, fearful and excited, their eyes wide with wonder. Any slight move on his part sent them scampering and giggling away. Only for a short distance, of course. The prisoner was obviously helpless and harmless.

He smiled at the children. This brought forth a flurry of conversation, more giggles, and a closer approach. One boy of perhaps ten summers advanced slowly and carefully, and reached to touch the prisoner's legging. A quick touch and a quicker retreat, amid a burst of excited laughter. He smiled at them again, and one very small girl returned his smile as their eyes met.

The game ended abruptly when an older woman approached, scolding and shooing the children away. She glanced at him with thinly veiled hostility and hurried on.

The pretty girl who had befriended him came with water in a gourd, and he drank. Her hands were gentle and caring. He wished that his own hands were free, so that he could communicate with her.

"I do not even know your name, Pretty One," he said aloud in his own tongue. He knew that she could not understand, but perhaps his tone would say what words could not. "I thank you for your help."

He was not certain how this girl related to what was happening to him, but he felt that she was very important to his welfare.

"I will talk to you tomorrow," she signed, as she turned away.

Now the village was quiet, the fires turning from red embers to gray-white ash. Everyone seemed to have forgotten the prisoner. He was just trying to determine whether he could sit or lie down within the limits of his fetters when he saw a figure approaching. He was startled, and afraid for a moment, helpless as he was. Then he saw that it was the chief himself.

"Bear Paws, I will take you to my lodge," the man signed.

With a great deal of confidence, he cut the thongs from the prisoner's hands.

There was a moment when Strong Bow, now Bear Paws, thought of attacking his captor and trying to make his escape. But he was stiff, his muscles weak. Besides, the man called Red Hand had been assigned to kill him in such an event. And he did not know where that one might be. He abandoned the idea, at least for now, and shuffled in the indicated direction, his steps short and halting because of the hobbles on his feet.

18
>> >> >>

Bear Paws stripped the ears of corn from the stalk, quickly checked to make certain he had not missed any, and moved on to the next. Slightly ahead of him, Kills-Three worked in the row to his right. A few steps behind, and to his left, Pretty Sky did the same.

He glanced back over his shoulder, and the girl smiled. He felt that he owed her much . . . his life, probably. It had been several sleeps, now, since the terrifying night of the celebration and council. He was still not certain what had transpired, but he gathered that his status was stable for now. He was sure that the girl who had befriended him was largely responsible, and he was grateful.

He was unsure about the girl's mother, Kills-Three. He had no knowledge of how the woman might have earned the name, and was not certain that he wished to know. The woman gave him a shove or a whack sometimes, but that was to be expected. After all, he was a prisoner. The blows were not in a vengeful spirit, but merely to assert her authority. He could understand that. After all, it was probably necessary to show the others that they were taking proper care of the prisoner.

Bear Paws had had little contact with Lone Elk, the girl's father, since the night of the council. He seemed stern, but not overly unfriendly. Strong Bow was made to think that this was a clever leader. He had sensed the quiet manipulation in the chief's words that night. A leader is best who seems to let others lead, he thought. And now, the prisoner was still a controversial figure. To maintain his effectiveness, Lone Elk must appear detached, retain at least the appearance of neutrality.

One thing had been quite worrisome. Red Hand, one of those who had seemed involved in the argument over the prisoner, watched him constantly. It was not that the man's presence was threatening in any way. It was only that he was always there, watching, waiting. Bear Paws would glance up from whatever task he had been assigned, and encounter the gaze of the warrior. It was not malevolent or vengeful. That might have been easier. But Red Hand only watched.

It was not so with Pumpkin Rings. The woman exuded a hate so strong that when she came near, he felt it, like a wave of anger. Or maybe, he thought, like the chill of a sudden shift in the wind, when Cold Maker creeps down from his lodge in the northern mountains to herald the coming winter. At any rate, it always sent a chill up his spine, and made the tiny hairs prickle along the back of his neck. The woman did nothing to conceal her enmity. In fact, she always made it a point to leer suggestively at him, and to make obscene gestures. She always allowed her glance to rest on his breechclout, and managed to draw her knife. She would absently test its keen edge with the ball of her thumb, while smiling her horrible, humorless smile at him. That was quite disconcerting, though he tried not to let it appear so.

Then there was the jokester. Laughing Crow was his name, Bear Paws had learned. That one, who had brought the severed head of the Spanish priest as a grim joke, because there was no scalp . . . Pretty Sky had explained it. Crow was always quite jovial when they encountered each other.

"Good day to you, my friend," Laughing Crow would sign. "Take good care of your hair, for it is mine!"

It was impossible to take the man seriously, despite his proven ability as a killer. That seemed completely out of character for Laughing Crow.

"I will do my best to keep it so," Bear Paws would answer.

This joke was gaining popularity, and the exchange was becoming an expected thing, perhaps as cherished as that of the nonexistent scalp. Bear Paws determined to do his best to keep the joke going. It is hard to kill a person who makes you laugh.

His first few days with the Horn People had been difficult, of course. He had not been certain of anything, and death might come anytime, at the next moment. He was still in the process of seeing that the scalp joke *was* a joke, and it was an ever present threat.

That first night after the celebration had ended, Lone Elk took him to their lodge. Not inside, of course. The prisoner was firmly tied to a post near the lodge door. That was his customary place now. The weather was warm, but nights became chilled and damp from the fog along the river. On the second night he was given a tattered buffalo robe, and slept more comfortably.

He had tried to understand as much as he could of the strange customs of these people. It was still a puzzle to him that they were growers, yet able hunters and warriors. His purpose in wanting to know more of their ways and their tongue was a simple one: If he understood them better, he could more easily guess his own fate.

Yet there was another motive in his thoughts. As he learned their ways, he could more easily devise a plan of escape.

He was helped considerably in his learning process by the girl, Pretty Sky. She seemed friendly, concerned over his welfare, and generally helpful. It was good. At first he was bothered by the red face-paint that was used by all of the women, but in a remarkably short time, it began to seem not unusual. And despite the face-paint, there was no denying that here was a beautiful young woman.

Bear Paws was convinced that it was largely at her demand that his hands had been freed. He was still hobbled, and no one made a move to change that. But with his hands free, he could begin to communicate, to learn some of their words.

"How are you called?" he signed. It was one of his first questions.

"I am Pretty Sky," the girl answered.

"It is good."

She smiled, showing even white teeth.

"What are your sounds for this?" he asked.

She told him, and he repeated the words aloud, rolling the unfamiliar syllables clumsily over his tongue.

"Pretty Sky."

She laughed, a delighted little chuckle, like that of a child with a new toy.

"And you are Bear Paws."

"Bear Paws," he repeated.

More laughter, and a pleased nod of the head.

"Will you teach me more of your tongue?" he asked in signs.

"Of course," she signed eagerly.

And so it had begun. Each learning session was short, because it was apparent that Kills-Three did not entirely approve. The woman was more concerned with assigning him menial tasks to do. He scraped a deerskin, ground corn, and gathered firewood. His fettered feet had been a problem in that activity at first. The short steps required by the hobbles did not lend themselves well to covering the distances required for gathering fuel.

Since the prisoner seemed cooperative, however, the hobbles were removed in a few days. There had been a serious discussion, which Bear Paws could not follow, and Lone Elk came over to the prisoner.

"We will take off the ties," he signed. "You know that Red Hand will kill you if you try to run away."

Bear Paws nodded.

The removal of the hobbles was a mixed blessing. He was now able to move more freely, but this made him eligible for more of the menial tasks of the grower. It was time for the harvesting of corn. Bear Paws, as Strong Bow, a child of the People, had eaten corn all his life, of course. He had seen the People trade meat and robes to the Growers for such commodities. He had no real idea, however, how corn was harvested and prepared for storage.

Now he was learning, firsthand. He had never realized that there were several types of corn. Some were gathered late in the season, to be stored in the ear, already well dried. These would be ground for meal, as his pueblo relatives had done for many lifetimes.

The crop which was the source of his current effort, however, was gathered while still soft. The green husks were stripped away, and the sweet, milky kernels sliced from the cob to be dried for storage.

He was learning more about such things than he wanted to know. The tasks started with gathering the ears in the field. That seemed easy enough, but before long his hands became sore. The swelling that had given him the Bear Paws name had gone down now, leaving his hands nearly normal. But they were the hands of a hunter, not those of a grower. The calluses were in the wrong places. There was a spot near the knuckle of his left index finger that was hardened by countless rubbings of an arrow shaft as it left the bow. Corresponding calluses from the feathered end of the shaft hardened spots on his right index finger. None of these protected his hands from the round serrated edges of the corn leaves. After half a day of picking, his hands and forearms were crisscrossed with tiny scratches which became quite uncomfortable. By evening, his hands were almost bleeding.

How long would it take, he wondered, to harden the skin to do such tasks? He wondered at the others. The rough leaves did not seem to affect the hands and arms of the others in the field. At least, not to this extent. Was there something different about their skin? He tried to look closely at the skin of Pretty Sky. As far as he could see, it looked soft and supple . . . Somehow the rough-edged blades did not seem to reach out, to encircle the shapely arm as it did his own. What . . . ?

Finally it came to him. He was not attuned to the spirit of the corn. He was as ill-suited for this, he thought to himself, as old Pumpkin Rings would be on a buffalo horse, running with the herd and shooting arrows at the fleeing quarry. So, what could one do?

If a person wished to become a buffalo hunter, it was necessary to become one with the spirit of the horse and the buffalo. It was a union of the spirits that produced the results. Could it be that it was the same with something like this? Like picking corn? It seemed incredible, and it had never occurred to him that he would *want* to become united with the spirits of the corn. Still, his grandparents must have done so. If it would keep the slashing edges of the corn blades from injuring his skin, it would be well worthwhile. He would try it tomorrow.

It helped greatly, too, when evening finally came and he was allowed to sit and rest. Pretty Sky came to him with a gourd that contained a greasy substance. She motioned that he should rub it on his skin. It smelled like buffalo fat, but there were other hints of pungent herbs and oils. It was soothing to spread on his burning hands, a strange mixture of hot and cold sensation. Maybe an application tomorrow, *before* he went to the field. He would ask. Just now, he was tired, and would sleep the dreamless sleep of exhaustion.

He wolfed down the food that he had been given . . . Better quality than at first. Kills-Three replaced his hobbles, but he did not care. He was too tired to think of trying to escape. Someday, he would, of course. He *would* escape. That was the only honorable plan for a man of the People, held prisoner and reduced to the degrading tasks of a woman of the growers. *Aiee,* he *must* escape. Later . . . He drifted off to sleep, only dimly aware of the murmur of the stream and the call of *Kookooskoos,* the owl, in the distance.

19

>> >> >>

Summer gave way to autumn, and there were new tasks for Bear Paws. He found himself doing things that he would never have considered until now. He ground corn, shelled beans, and now, late in the Moon of Harvest, he sliced pumpkins.

For the People, this was the Moon of Hunting, for they were not harvesters. For these Horn People, with their strange ways, both names were used. He was certain, after this experience, that he would always remember it as the Moon of Harvest. If, of course, he lived to see another such season. It was still plain that there were those whose goal was to see that he did not.

He was not really mistreated, beyond the occasional whack with a stick when Kills-Three decided that he was not moving fast enough. His feet were no longer tied, but he was still watched closely. He now slept inside the lodge of Lone Elk.

That had happened late in the Red Moon. The weather was sweltering hot, and everyone was sleeping outside to catch any stirring of the air that might be available. The prisoner, of course, had never slept elsewhere. He still rolled in his robe outside the lodge each night. Then came a day of change, the change in the wind that his brother, the holy man, spoke of. It foretold a change in the weather, usually rain. By evening, the air was cool, almost uncomfortably so. Old people sought robes to put around their arthritic shoulders, and crouched over their fires.

The rain came just before dark, and there was a frantic scurry to bring everything inside. Bear Paws stood with his tattered sleeping robe over his head, listening to the drumming patter of the drops on the skin. At least, it would be some protection. He wondered if he would be expected to live outside during the winter snows. Surely he would freeze. It would not become a problem, of course, if they killed him before then. Either way, it looked like a bleak winter.

There was a sudden loud whack across his shoulders, as Kills-Three's stick landed on the wet skin.

"Come on, stupid!" she yelled at him.

That was one word he understood quite well. It was used almost as frequently as "Bear Paws." He peered out from under the robe. Kills-Three was motioning, pointing into the lodge door.

"Me?" he asked, dumfounded.

"Of course, stupid. Come on!"

She hurried ahead of him, bending to enter. Bear Paws followed, with misgivings. A man should not live in a hole in the ground. The very thought gave him a trapped feeling. Fighting it down, he hurried after the woman.

It took a moment for his eyes to adjust to the dim interior. A roughly circular lodge, with a fire-pit in the center, and a small smoke-hole in the roof. Around the periphery was a low ledge or bench, with a variety of robes and other items lying on it. The floor was smooth and hard, of pounded clay. He learned that later. For now, he was thinking only that this cavelike structure was close, enclosing, suffocating. It smelled of animal scent, like the nest of a mouse under a log. Or maybe, like a bear's den.

He and a couple of playmates had found a bear's den once. It was a frightening thing. It was during his seventh summer. The den was abandoned, so there was no real danger, but the bear-smell was still present, a reminder that the creature had spent its winter sleep there. He and the others had fled in terror. His brother had laughed at them, but everyone knew that it was serious. Not because of any threat, but because of the trapped *feeling,* the dread of being enclosed, with no access to the open breeze, no path of escape.

It was so in this earth-lodge of the Pawnees. The vague, indefinable odor of human sweat and habitation came at him in an overpowering wave. It was not entirely unfamiliar, of course. A skin-lodge came to smell like this in the winter, with dry grass stuffed behind the lining for warmth, and snow banked around the outside to stop Cold Maker's chilling breath. The collective body scents would build up. It was always a relief, in the Moon of Awakening, to raise the edge of the lodge-skin on a sunny day and let the spring breeze cleanse the air.

That was impossible here. Bear Paws was tempted to turn and flee outside again, into the chill of the rain. At least, it *smelled* better. But he must remain calm. His continued survival depended on it.

Kills-Three pointed to a spot on the ledge, and moved some small articles to make a space.

"Me?" he signed, asking permission to approach.

The woman nodded. "Put your robe there!" she signed.

So, Bear Paws had moved into the lodge of Lone Elk and Kills-Three. He was not accepted as a member of the lodge, of course. He still slept outside whenever the weather permitted. Kills-Three made the decision each time, and sometimes the prisoner disagreed. Toward morning, on a frosty night, for instance, the warmth of the lodge seemed desirable as he shivered under his moth-eaten buffalo robe.

The woman's attitude seemed to soften toward him, however, as the days passed. He was actually approaching the point where he felt that he could request permission to enter the lodge.

It still bothered him greatly that there was no escape from such a lodge in case of attack. In the skin-lodges of the People, one could lift the lower edge of the lodge cover and roll under it into the open, to fight or run. Gradually, he came to understand some of the factors involved here. One was that an enemy, entering an earth-lodge, would be at a decided disadvantage. The intruder would be stooping, head bowed, and vulnerable to a blow from anyone inside. He could not see the blow coming, either. And the intruder would also be alone. Only one could enter such a lodge at a time.

Bear Paws' other realization was not so reassuring. He had been assigned a place on the sleeping-ledge just inside the entrance. In the event of an intruder, he would be the nearest to the attack. Lone Elk and Kills-Three slept opposite the doorway, beyond the fire. They would have time to defend themselves while those nearer the door fell victim . . . He wondered again how the woman had earned her name. He was certain that she was worthy of it.

He was beginning to understand, too, more of the ways of these people. He was preparing pumpkins for drying one morning, slicing thin rings . . . *Aiee!* Rings. Pumpkin Rings. This was the origin of the name of the woman who wished to use her knife on him, too. Was she named that because she was adept at the use of the knife? He did not really want to think about that.

He continued slicing pumpkins, frequently criticized by Kills-Three.

"Cut them thinner! Those will rot instead of drying!"

He would nod and do as he was told, trying his best to please. After all, his life might depend on it. Slicing pumpkins for drying was not unlike slicing meat for the same purpose. A strip cut too thick would spoil, while a properly sliced portion would dry and keep almost indefinitely unless it became wet.

The pumpkin rings were strung on a thong, and stored, after drying, by hanging from the rafter poles that formed the ceiling of the lodge. They were so tough and leathery that it was hard to recognize their origin.

He was rapidly learning more words, too. At first, names, common words like *eat* and *water, knife, lodge.* Pretty Sky was his tutor. She seemed to take great pleasure in teaching him, and it was also pleasant for him.

"Why is your mother called 'Kills-Three'?" he signed one day.

"Because it is her name," was the reply.

"No, no. How did that come to be?"

"Oh. I do not know. I will ask . . ."

"No," he signed hastily. He did not feel, somehow, that such inquiry would be appropriate.

He used mostly hand-signs, despite his increasing knowledge of the Pawnee tongue. He might be able to learn more. If they thought him ignorant of the conversation they would talk more freely. He developed the habit of assuming a blank stare when a conversation was in progress, except when signs were used.

Even with Pretty Sky he did this. He felt a little guilty about it, for the girl seemed to be genuinely trying to help him. She already had, it appeared. He was still alive.

He had other feelings for her, however, that had nothing to do with gratitude. From his first sight of her, Bear Paws had realized that this was one of the most attractive women he had ever seen. Even her face-paint could not conceal that fact. The attraction was becoming stronger by the day. He longed to be near her, to touch her, to have her touch him.

It was quite frustrating. Bear Paws would lie awake in the lodge on a rainy night, and listen to the breathing of the others . . . the deep snores of Lone Elk, the more feminine sounds from Kills-Three, and the soft regular intake and expiration of breath from Pretty Sky, across the lodge. *Even her breathing is beautiful,* he thought. He longed to creep around the fire and approach her bed, to touch her . . . *Aiee!* He must avoid such thoughts, lest he get himself killed.

Even while such thoughts troubled his rest, he continued to think of escape. It was something that one must think of. From the time they were small, children of the People were taught pride in their heritage. If one is captured, the first thought is of survival. If one must die, let him do so with dignity. But if not, he does what he must to survive, and to return to the People.

There were inspiring stories of such courage in the legends. Children were told of Pale Star, kidnapped as a child and carried far away. She had grown up as a slave, and married twice before she returned to the People, bringing her second husband with her. She was among the most honored of women.

Or Horse Seeker . . . what an inspiring tale. His vision-quest took him far away. It had been necessary for him to spend a season among another nation, and to fight to retrieve the sacred Elk-dog medicine of the People, the Spanish bit worn by the First Horse.

A child, raised on such stories of pride and loyalty, does

not forget. One *must* escape and return to the tallgrass country of the Sacred Hills. So all his activities, his nebulous plans, revolved around this one goal. He began to plan how he could gather a small amount of food, to be ready to take with him at a moment's notice. A knife . . . That should be easy, because he used a knife for preparing pumpkins. His robe.

A factor that was disturbing to him was the season. Long lines of geese honked their way south across the clear blue of the autumn sky. There should be time, though, even granted that this was an area farther north than the People. He watched the changing of the season, the gold and purple of the autumn flowers, with mixed feelings. It was a season of the year that he loved, the crisp mornings and the ripe scents of fall. But it foretold winter, and he dare not try to travel then. No, his escape must be soon, or else he must resign himself to a winter in the closeness of an earth-lodge.

He could choose his time for escape, and travel due south as rapidly as possible. A few days should put him into more familiar country. Possibly country that was used by the Northern band of the People. He would ask the Growers where that band was wintering, and head there. They in turn could tell him of his own Southern band. Or, if need be, he could winter with the Northern band, and rejoin his own people at the Sun Dance next season. He hoped that he would be able to get word to his parents not to mourn.

There was one factor that added more to his confusion: Pretty Sky. His feelings for her were increasing daily. At times, in fantasy, he wondered if there was a possibility that she would go *with* him, back to the People. His dilemma, of course, was that he could not ask her. Even she must not be aware of his plans to escape.

Laughing Crow interrupted these thoughts as he passed by.

"Ho, Bear Paws, take good care of my hair!"

Bear Paws waved, smiling sheepishly.

"Of course! As long as I can!"

20
>> >> >>

There was one factor that disturbed Bear Paws in his plans for escape before the coming of winter. It was one over which he had no control whatever, yet one which held more threat to his success than any other. That factor was Pumpkin Rings. The others who held threats against his life had mellowed. Laughing Crow with his jokes about his ownership of the prisoner's scalp had become no threat. He was almost a friend, a source of mutual humor. Even Red Hand, who claimed the right to kill him, seemed in no hurry. That one had watched closely at first. There would have been no hesitation to kill, Bear Paws was sure. But now, Red Hand seemed to pay little attention to him.

He must make sure, after the escape, of course. Red Hand would be the one who would track him relentlessly to the end. At least, if anyone did. Bear Paws wondered some about that. He had now become so much a part of the daily routine of the village that he wondered. It would be tempting, he thought, if Red Hand did follow him, to try to bargain. Maybe he could talk his way out of a fight. If not . . . well, so be it. He had no qualms about fighting Red Hand.

Another thought occurred to him. Maybe he could offer to fight Red Hand openly, here in the village. The outcome could determine whether he would be permitted to leave. It would be an event of great amusement for the other members of the town. In the end, he decided against such an approach. It was too risky. It would have been acceptable, even desirable, among the Head Splitters or the People, for a prisoner to suggest this. But he was unsure of the ways of these people. Besides, why ask for trouble where there is none? This offer would alert everyone to his desire to leave, and he would be watched more closely. He had gone to great lengths to conceal his plans for escape. Why, then, should he reveal the wish? In the end, he rejected the idea of a challenge.

But there was still the old woman to deal with. From the first day, he had viewed her with dread. If it had not been for the intervention of Lone Elk, he would have been converted very slowly and painfully into smaller pieces that day, he was sure. Yet while the others of the village had moderated in their attitude toward the prisoner, the mood of Pumpkin Rings seemed the opposite. Laughing Crow and even Red Hand were quite tolerant of his presence, but the woman . . . *Aiee!* It was frightening.

He could understand, of course. The warriors regarded him simply as a defeated enemy. Maybe, even, as one who had merely been unfortunate enough to be *with* the enemy. They held no grudges. Pumpkin Rings, however, held the prisoner solely responsible for her shattered life. He was sorry for her losses. Of the few deaths from the battle with the Spanish, how odd that two were father and son.

What he could not understand was that Pumpkin

Rings persisted in placing the blame on him. He had not even been there at the time. He was already a prisoner. He made one attempt to communicate with the woman, but she flew into a violent rage. He withdrew, puzzled.

"Let her alone," advised Pretty Sky. "She is a little crazy, maybe, with grief."

"But her losses . . . I had nothing to do with that!"

"I know. But she will not see that. Just avoid her."

That was hard to do. The old woman followed him, sometimes close, sometimes at a distance. Would she follow, he wondered, when he carried out his plans to leave? He dreamed one night that he had escaped, and was traveling across a wide rolling prairie. Yet every time he looked back, there was the dreaded figure with her ever present knife. He had awakened in a cold sweat.

He would steal a horse, he decided. One of the best. Maybe his own, now claimed by Red Hand. Yes . . . that would slow the pursuit. Red Hand would have to choose a lesser animal, one which would probably be slower. Then it would be easy to outdistance an old woman on foot, too. Yes, that would be a part of the plan. Much better to run from the threat of the bitter old widow than to have to kill her on the trail.

He was growing in confidence now. It would be a matter of timing, when to leave, for best traveling before the cold weather. He judged the seasons to be not too different from those of the People. It would soon be the Moon of Falling Leaves. There should be another moon of good weather for travel, at least.

The harvest was nearly complete, and there had been a fall buffalo hunt. Bear Paws had not been permitted to participate, of course. He had been amused at the scope of the hunt. It was a small thing, compared to the gigantic forays against the great herds that were carried out by the People. But in a sense, the atmosphere was present. There was the work of drying meat and dressing hides, which was familiar to him. Now things were quieter, and there was a sense of fruition, of completeness in the year. There had been religious ceremonies, which he did not understand and did not wish to, except as an interesting diversion.

At about this time, a party from one of the other towns stopped by for a visit. Bear Paws was surprised when one of them sought him out. The man looked familiar, but it took a moment to make the identification. It was the storyteller who had shared the campfire . . . Ah, how long ago it seemed now! Another time, another world.

"I heard you were here," the man signed. "Are you telling stories?"

Bear Paws laughed, a little bitterly. "No, Uncle. I am fortunate to be alive."

"True. But you must keep the skills alive. You were good with the stories. This may be of help to you."

Memory came creeping back. This man had seemed familiar with the Creation story of the People.

"Uncle," he signed, "you knew my stories. *How?*"

The old man chuckled.

"*I* was a prisoner of *your* people, once," he signed. "For a season. I escaped."

"You . . . Then you know my tongue?"

They had been conversing in hand-signs until now, but Bear Paws spoke aloud in the tongue of the People.

The old man shook his head. "No, no," he signed. "That was long ago. I knew only a little, then. But I remembered your stories. The fat woman . . ." He chuckled again. "What will you do?" he asked suddenly.

Bear Paws was almost caught off guard. He had been conversing with a pleasant person who understood some of the customs of home. Now, the question had been thrown at him, about his plans. Was that the purpose of this conversation? To find whether he was preparing to escape? Surely not. This was a man with whom he had much in common. Yet it would be foolhardy to say too much.

"A prisoner has no plans, Uncle," he signed cautiously. "Only what he is permitted."

The old man nodded seriously, but there was a twinkle of understanding in his eye.

"Be careful of the woman."

"What woman?" Bear Paws asked innocently.

Now the old storyteller laughed aloud.

"Both of them."

"Both?"

This was an unexpected turn of events. He had only been trying to profess his nonunderstanding, to appear more innocent than he was, to allay suspicion. What other woman should he avoid?

"Of course," the other signed. "The old woman with the knife, and the pretty young one."

He turned and walked away, still chuckling.

Bear Paws looked after him. Was there a woman of the People, perhaps of the Northern band, who had befriended this man? What was their relationship? This made his own situation seem more complicated than it actually was.

He turned aside, still disturbed. How had the old man managed to know of his fantasies about Pretty Sky? This was irritating. If a casual visitor could see that there was something there, how many others were also aware? And how would it affect his escape?

Wait . . . No, this was good. He had convinced himself that the most important thing was the escape. If there were those who thought in terms of a budding romance, they would be less likely to suspect his real plans.

Yes, it was good! Better than he had thought, in fact. He would play along, would show interest in the girl.

Then there would be complete surprise when he disappeared.

As if in answer to his thought, Pretty Sky approached. It was a beautiful evening, just a touch of chill in the air, and a few scattered clouds.

"Come," she said, in signs and in her tongue, "let us watch the sunset."

They crossed the shallows and walked to a little rise. Sun Boy . . .

"My people would say Sun Boy chooses his paints well tonight," he signed.

She laughed, her pleasant chuckling laughter. The sky was streaked with crimson and gold and purple, stretching almost around the rim of the earth.

"It is good," she signed.

And it *was* good. They stayed and watched until the last crimson streaks in the west faded to purple. The moon rose behind them, and she leaned against his shoulder.

Aiee, he thought. *Maybe the old storyteller knows things I do not.* His life seemed to become more complicated all the time.

21

>> >> >>

Pretty Sky watched from a distance as Bear Paws talked with old Lame Heron, the storyteller from the western towns. She was a bit disturbed at the conversation. It was good that they talked, of course. She wanted the captive to adjust to the culture of her people, to be comfortable in it. Only then could her plan for him—for herself—work well.

What concerned her was the seriousness and length of the conversation. The two seemed to *know* each other. How could this be? The storyteller, it was known, had once been a captive of some tribe to the south . . . No, that was long ago, a time of another generation, before she was born. And, of course, before Bear Paws was born. But there was something. She could sense it in their attitude, the position of their bodies as they talked, both in hand-signs and words. They were a little too far away for her to follow the signs. Maybe she should move closer.

"What is it, Sky?" her mother interrupted her thoughts.

"What? Oh . . . Mother. I was watching Bear Paws and the old man, there."

"Watching what?"

"Well, look . . . It is as if they know each other. They are talking."

Kills-Three laughed.

"They will not talk much. Bear Paws knows little of our tongue."

"But he is good with signs. And watch a moment, Mother."

There was a pause, while Kills-Three observed.

"Yes . . . It does appear so. Well, they *have* met before."

"Really?" If Pretty Sky had known that, she had forgotten.

"Yes. The Spanish spent a night with one of the western towns. This Bear Paws told stories with old Heron. Do you not remember?"

"Ah, yes, I do now, Mother," Pretty Sky laughed.

She had made a problem where there was none. At least it seemed so. Of course the captive would enjoy seeing a friendly face. His life had been hard since she had first seen him, bound hand and foot, and miserable in his captivity.

Her mother had not entirely approved of her interest in the prisoner, but had agreed to help her. Pretty Sky's heart had gone out to the young man, so proud in his tormented condition, facing death with courage. That possibility was more remote now. Even so, old Pumpkin Rings was a danger, possibly more than Bear Paws realized. The woman was a little crazy, Sky thought. Actually, a little crazy even before the tragic loss of her son and husband. A number of times, Pretty Sky had almost decided to warn Bear Paws against the old woman's treachery. But he seemed to recognize it. He would be careful.

A more pressing fear to her now was whether the prisoner would try to escape. At first that had not been a great risk. She had helped to persuade her father that Bear Paws would not be dangerous, and to free his bonds. That had proved true. Yet, in helping him to achieve this much freedom, she had provided him the means to escape if he chose.

And she did not want him to leave. Initially, she had felt only pity for him, as she would for an injured creature, or a fledgling bird, perhaps. She had once encountered a young hawk, fresh from the nest and unable to fly more than a few paces. When approached, the bird would turn on its tormentors with a startling hiss and a proud warning stare. The children had kept their distance, well aware of the damage that could be done by the slashing beak and talons. Yes, her feeling for this prisoner had been much like that, and she had tried to help him, though she was afraid.

Gradually, her attitude had changed. The pity had changed to admiration, as she saw him adapt to a harsh situation with courage and good humor. She had been pleased with his reaction to Laughing Crow's claim on his scalp. Bear Paws had shown no fear, and his part of the continuing joke was respected and admired. Yes, here was a man she could appreciate.

She was attracted to him physically, of course. More than she admitted openly. His features were handsome, his body tall and strong, broad-shouldered and with well-muscled arms. Strong Bow, he had said he was called in his own tongue. A good name, well chosen. It made little difference now, of course. He was Bear Paws to her people.

And now, her primary goal for Bear Paws was no longer to save his life, but to *keep* him. If she could prevent his leaving before winter . . . if he could spend the long winter nights in the lodge with her and her family, she could induce him to stay, she was sure. Of course, since he was a prisoner, she could demand that he sleep with her, or marry her. But she wanted him to *want* to. Her goal was a more lasting relationship.

So, she worked slowly and deliberately. She must not push him too fast. He was adapting well to the customs of her people. Her fear was that as he made this adaptation, he was achieving more freedom of movement. This would enable him to escape more easily if he chose.

And if he did, one of those who threatened his life might kill him. Pumpkin Rings or Red Hand . . . it mattered little. He would be just as dead either way. Sometimes she thought that she *wanted* him to escape. An odd thought, but she understood it. She had come to have such strong feelings for this young man . . . Here there was ever present danger to him. If he was not killed by one of his enemies, he might be by another. If he escaped, and managed to elude those who would do him harm, he would be lost to her, but would live.

She sighed.

"What is it, pretty one?" her mother asked.

The girl hesitated a moment, and then answered.

"I . . . I do not know, Mother. I am afraid he will try to leave."

"Afraid he will be killed?"

"Yes, that also. But it would be better if he wants to stay."

Kills-Three chuckled. There had been a time long ago, before she earned her imposing name, when she had been as beautiful as Sky. All the eyes of the young men had followed her, as they now followed her daughter. One season follows another.

"Then you must make him want to stay."

"What?"

"Make him *want* to. This life must look more attractive to him than that which he left."

Pretty Sky was startled.

"But, Mother . . ."

"Yes, you can do this. You have an advantage, the strange and unknown promise, a thing he cannot find with his own people."

"H-how?" the girl stammered.

Kills-Three looked at the sky. Clumps of fluffy white clouds drifted lazily across the pure blue. A near-perfect autumn day, with shadows already growing long.

"Well, look," she told her daughter. "The day is fine. There should be a brilliant sunset. Take him . . . there, that rise to the south. Watch the colors, talk about that, and the geese, ask him of his childhood. Must I tell you *everything* to do?"

Pretty Sky giggled. She had never thought of her mother as romantic. She was seeing a new side to this stern parent.

"No, Mother. Some things I can do for myself. But thank you!"

She hurried away, to fix her hair and renew her face-paint. There was a little time before the flaming display of sun and sky and clouds would begin.

Bear Paws did not seem to object to her suggestion. They walked to the little rise and watched the colors mingle and shift and change, saying very little. Only as the last red-orange streaks along Earth's rim faded did they begin to talk.

She was surprised that he knew so much of her tongue. He must have listened carefully and remembered everything. When there came a difficulty in understanding, they resorted to signs, laughing even as they did so.

The moon rose behind them, huge and red.

"A Harvest Moon," she told him.

"But my people would say a *Hunter's* Moon," he reminded.

Both laughed. They were finding things amusing that were really not. Or had not been until now.

An owl in the trees along the stream sounded his hollow cry, and another answered.

"*Kookooskoos!*" Bear Paws said.

"What?"

"That is his name, for my people. He calls his own name."

She laughed, the delightful sound that he found so attractive.

A coyote called in the distance.

"What is his name?" she asked.

"Little Wolf, in my tongue."

"And what does *he* say?"

"Nothing. He only laughs at the behavior of humans."

The girl laughed at that, and asked more such questions. They talked of many things . . . how the coyote stole fire from the Sun for the use of mankind. How the bobcat lost his tail.

He was a good storyteller, and it flattered him to have an appreciative audience. She kept the tales going with her questions. The night air became chilled, and they unconsciously clung closer together to share the warmth of young bodies. Maybe, of course, it was not entirely unconscious.

They stayed a long time. By the time they walked down the slope, arms around each other's waists, the moon was high. It was no longer large and red, but small and silvery white now. They splashed across the shallows and quietly made their way to the lodge. The entire village seemed bright as day, silvered by the moon's pale light. It was a night to be remembered, a special time that they had shared.

She gave his hand a little squeeze as they parted, Bear

Paws to seek his bed at the right of the entrance, Pretty
Sky to her own, across the lodge. They were very quiet,
hoping not to waken the sleepers.

The deep snore of Lone Elk droned on, undisturbed.
The sounds of Kills-Three's breathing were fainter, but
regular. In a few moments the young people were settled quietly, and the lodge was still, except for the sounds
of sleep.

In the darkness, Kills-Three smiled with satisfaction. It
was quite late, so the evening must have gone well with
Pretty Sky and her plans. She drifted off to sleep now,
thinking of the thrill and excitement of young love.

22
>> >> >>

Bear Paws judged that it was yet some time before dawn. Now that the morning of decision had come, he wondered whether he had the courage to carry out his plan. The results, successful or not, would be so permanent.

Yet, he felt that it was imperative he make his move. He had been deeply affected by the moonlit night on the knoll. When he awoke that next morning he was astonished at how easily he had slipped into acceptance of the situation as it now stood.

Pretty Sky had smiled knowingly at him, and he was almost overcome with a rush of mixed feelings. It was pleasing and flattering to be the object of such attention. What man could long refuse the advances of such a beautiful young woman? There was a strong temptation to accept this as the way that he wanted things to be. It became even easier in the next little while, as the family rose and began to move around the lodge.

It was not until later that day that he stopped to think

about it, and realized the change in his attitude. There was nothing specific to call his attention. He had gone upstream a little way to look for firewood. Some familiar sight or sound, some smell, perhaps . . . Maybe a combination. He had simply emerged from a clump of willows into a little meadow. Three horses were grazing there. One lifted its head and spoke to him, the soft snuffling sound that a mare uses to reassure her foal.

His attention was distracted from the task at hand, and he lifted his eyes to look beyond. A vast span of prairie stretched before him, gently rolling in its form. In the far reaches of his gaze, a range of low hills was blue with distance, and misty with the haze of autumn. It reminded him of the sacred Tallgrass Hills of his people, and the shock stopped him in his tracks. *What am I doing?* he asked himself. How could he even think of staying here? Even with the incentive provided by the beautiful girl . . . *Aiee,* he was a man of the open prairie. He must not allow himself to even consider the unthinkable. How could he, if the occasion ever offered, explain to his family? How could a man of the People become one who lived in a hole in the ground? Could he watch his sons and daughters grow up in such a culture, painting their faces red and plastering their hair with tallow to form a horn?

Panic gripped him. He must escape! For a moment, he considered leaping on the horse and riding like mad toward the distant hills. *Wait,* he told himself. *That is foolish. Be calm. Plan carefully.*

By the time he returned to the village, his thoughts were under control. True, he must escape, but not madly and foolishly. He would plan, as he had already begun to do. There was now new urgency, however. Not only from the weather and the coming change of seasons, but from this new dilemma. He was certain that he could not

long withstand the sort of persuasion that Pretty Sky was
well equipped to offer.

So, it was time to go. It was a few days before his plans
were complete. He had effectively scouted the routine
activity of the buffalo horse that he would use. He knew
exactly the little meadow along the stream where Red
Hand would have the animal picketed. His small packet
of dried meat, light and easy to carry, was ready, con-
cealed in a fold of his robe.

And now, the time had come. He had not slept. Several times during the early part of the night, he almost
lost his resolve. The deep breathing of the girl across the
room . . . *Aiee,* he must not think of such things! He
tried to put out of his mind the warm softness of her body
next to his, her caresses . . .

Now, the breathing of all three others in the lodge was
quiet and regular. Now was the time. He must make this
as natural as possible, in case anyone awoke. He must
appear to be merely going out to empty his bladder. He
slid off the ledge and shuffled into his moccasins quietly
yet trying not to appear secretive. He rose and shuffled
to the door and hesitated as if befuddled by sleep. Then
he turned back to pick up his robe. It was a logical action,
because the nights were chill, and the mornings touched
with frost now.

At the door, he paused to draw the robe around his
shoulders and to listen a moment. There was no sound
except the regular breathing. He pushed the hanging
door-skin aside and stepped through quickly, letting the
skin fall back into place. He straightened and took a deep
breath of the frosty night air.

Although there was a chill to the dark night, his palms
were damp with sweat. Would he really be able to do it?
He must not think such thoughts . . . He glanced at the
sky . . . The Seven Hunters were farther around their

nightly sweep than he had expected. He must hurry, but not appear to do so, in case he was watched.

He strolled over to the appropriate area, trying hard to be casual, and proceeded to empty his bladder. If he had been seen, this would throw the pursuit off track. Then he stood there a moment, after rearranging his breechclout, listening for any signs that anyone else was stirring. A dark figure came slowly toward him, and he gripped his knife, but then relaxed. It was only an old man, out of his lodge for the same ostensible purpose as Bear Paws. The man mumbled a sleepy greeting and Bear Paws responded with the same, hoping devoutly that his act would be accepted. The other, who seemed only half awake, gave no indication of suspicion, so Bear Paws moved on, heading back toward the lodges.

Once out of sight, he diverted his course and headed for the riffle. He had previously experimented there, searching out the portion of the riffle that would be the most quiet to cross. There were fewer slippery rounded stones here to cause one to lose footing.

He glanced at the sky again. There was a yellow-gray smudge in the east, already heralding the false dawn. His plan was running late . . . Should he go back? No, he must go, now, or face the possibility that he might not go at all.

He jogged downstream to the little meadow where the horse would be, and stopped to locate the animal. It was nowhere to be seen. Perhaps in the willows by the stream . . . Frantically, he trotted along, peering into the dark shrubbery, but he was met with failure.

"Huh!" he exclaimed softly to himself. What had happened? Did the horse wander off? Had Red Hand decided to picket the animal elsewhere? The grass was still good here. Why would . . . *Aiee!* Had Red Hand guessed his plan, and picketed the horse where it would

be unavailable to the fugitive? A prickling chill crept up his spine.

It was a moment of decision. He must find a horse, *any* horse, very quickly, or give up the entire thought of escape, at least for now. The band of yellow in the east was becoming more prominent now, and stars began to fade. Objects began to appear more clearly, ghostly in the deceptive light.

There was a rustle in the brush near him . . . Ah, the horse . . . He hurried toward the sound, then stopped short. The figure that rose out of the darkness was not animal, but human. He was close now, and even in the dim predawn light he could recognize Pumpkin Rings. She held her knife at ready.

"Red Hand!" she called. "I have him here."

Another figure rose a few paces away, and a third in another area. Laughing Crow . . . They had guessed! Probably old Pumpkin Rings had spied on him, and alerted the others. It was over. He was defeated, and now he shuddered to think of the results. He had been an idiot. He could have snuggled in for the winter with a warm-bodied and sensuous wife. Instead, he now faced a horrible death by torture.

"Mother, I . . ." he began helplessly.

"Silence, dog! I will give you reason to make noise. You will scream for me to stop!"

For a moment he considered turning to run, but it appeared useless. Already Red Hand was fitting an arrow to his string. Laughing Crow stood holding his bow, a look of something like sadness on his face in the dim light that was rapidly growing brighter. *He hates to lose his joke,* thought Bear Paws.

Yet another figure now rose, behind the three. Does everyone know? Then more . . . perhaps a dozen or more, flitting silently among the scattered dogwood and willow. The nearest held a bow, and was lifting it . . .

Aiee! These were not men of the village! Enemies . . .
He did not know what enemies might be feared by the
Horn People, but they were certainly about to be at-
tacked.

"Look out!" he cried. "Behind you!"

The old woman actually laughed aloud.

"An old trick, Bear Paws!"

Even as she spoke, he watched the nearest warrior
raise his weapon. It seemed a long time, as the arrow
point rose and swung, and the string twanged. He felt so
helpless . . . The air was filled with the soft buzz of
arrows now, as other attackers poured down the low
slope toward them.

Laughing Crow was the first to fall, struck from behind
by the first arrow. Bear Paws jumped forward, diving
toward Crow's weapon to defend himself. The attackers,
he realized, would as soon kill him . . . They had no
way to know that he was a prisoner. He grasped the bow
and a couple of arrows that had fallen from the quiver.
Even as he fitted an arrow to the string and rose to one
knee to search for a target, he was yelling. By pure reflex
he found himself voicing at the top of his lungs the deep,
full-throated war cry of the People.

He saw Pumpkin Rings fall, struck down by a thrown
ax. Red Hand was fighting for his life, loosing two arrows
before he was forced to drop the bow and reach for his
belt-ax.

Bear Paws launched his first arrow at Red Hand's attacker, but could not see if it struck. He, too, was hard-
pressed. His next arrow struck a charging warrior, and
his third missed. That attacker was on him in an instant,
and he flung the bow into the man's face, giving him the
space of a heartbeat or two to draw his knife. It sank
deep into the soft midriff of his adversary and the two
went down together. This probably saved the life of Bear
Paws, as an attacker's musket boomed. He felt the ball

whistle past his head as he fell. He rolled, shoving the body aside to rush at the warrior with the empty musket. The man turned and fled, and Bear Paws voiced the People's war cry again.

Now men were pouring out of the village. In the brightening day it could be seen that the attackers were in confusion. Some were retreating, others still attacking. They had been surprised by the ready resistance. There was a crackle of musket fire from the direction of the village, and now the enemy was in full retreat. A warrior or two turned to fire as they fled.

Bear Paws saw a cottony puff of smoke from a distant musket, and felt something pluck at his left arm. A moment later the boom of the weapon reached his ears. He looked down in surprise to see the trickle of blood down his buckskin sleeve. He was wounded . . . It would take a short while for the pain to begin.

He looked down at the fallen Laughing Crow, and found him alive, looking up with a puzzled expression. Crow's chances of survival did not look good.

Now a wave of weakness washed over him, and Bear Paws sat down beside the fallen Crow.

"Bear Paws," whispered Crow, "take care of my hair!"

Bear Paws' head was swimming, and he found it hard to focus his eyes.

"As long as I can," he managed to mutter.

People were running now, looking after the wounded, counting casualties, and taking enemy weapons and scalps. Pretty Sky dropped to her knees beside Bear Paws.

"You are bleeding!" she cried. "Here, let me tie it."

She cut away the sleeve, tightly wrapping the arm with the help of her mother, to stop the bleeding.

"It went through the soft meat," Kills-Three announced. "It is good."

Bear Paws had some doubts about that, but had to admit that things could be worse. At least, he was alive.

"What about Laughing Crow?" he asked.

"Dead," Kills-Three said simply. "How did you know of the attack?"

Bear Paws hesitated. It was hard to think . . . especially when he had no answer.

"I . . ." he began. "Mother, I did not . . ."

"He did *not* know," stated Red Hand from behind her.

So, now it was really over, Bear Paws realized. Red Hand would tell of his attempted escape. The warrior stepped around to face him.

"Bear Paws became suspicious, and discovered the enemy," Red Hand declared. "He tried to warn Pumpkin Rings and Crow, but they would not listen to him."

Bear Paws sat there, unable to comprehend.

"But I . . ." he stammered.

"He gave the war cry that woke the village and spread the warning," Red Hand went on, "and he took Crow's weapon after he fell . . . Bear Paws saved *my* life!"

Blackness was creeping over his consciousness. So tired . . . He was barely aware of the murmur of approval from the onlookers.

23
>> >> >>

South Wind lifted the lodge lining and shoved her armful of grass into the space between it and the skin cover. She paused to rearrange a couple of rawhide storage bags, and then let the lining drop back into place. A few more trips, a little more stuffing, and she would consider the lodge ready for winter.

They were located well, with a thicket of scrub oak sheltering the north side of the camp. The fall hunt had been good. The children were fat and the women happy. But the heart of South Wind was very heavy. Her youngest son, the child of their old age, was missing. Strong Bow had not returned, and there was no word of him.

In the Moon of Hunting had come a message, passed on by a traveler who had stopped in the pueblo of their distant kinsmen. It was a common way to communicate, though not always the most accurate.

The party from Santa Fe, it was said, had been attacked by Pawnees on the Platte. Most of the Spanish had withdrawn and immediately started home. The retreating survivors had stopped at the pueblo of their kinsmen to tell of the debacle.

"But what of our son, Strong Bow?" South Wind demanded of the traveler.

The man spread his palms in dismay.

"I do not know, Mother. I am only telling it as it was told to me."

"They said nothing of a young Elk-dog man among the survivors?"

"I am trying to tell you . . . They spoke of this man, yes. But he was not with the hairfaces at the battle."

"He was *not?*"

If not there, then where *was* he? She wondered. It would not be surprising if he had come to his senses and left the Spanish expedition before the attack. That seemed the likeliest explanation. But after that, she would have expected him to come home. She tried to think where this battle may have been. Somewhere to the north, of course. Maybe northeast. And if the battle had been in the Red Moon, as it was told, Strong Bow should have been home by now. Long before now, actually. South Wind, knowing what a congenial type her son was, tried to allow for the fact that he would probably stop to visit relatives in the Northern or Eastern bands. Maybe hunt with them. Yes, the fall hunts would be in progress.

Eventually, though, she had to admit the truth. Even with these delays, he should have turned up before now. And to confirm her suspicions, there had been no word. There was always a certain amount of traveling between bands in the summer. Young people, spending part of the season with friends or relatives, maybe a joint hunting party.

So, South Wind had sent out inquiries. She had made good contacts with both Northern and Eastern bands, but Strong Bow had not been seen. Even the Growers, who traded with everyone and gathered news of all, had heard nothing.

The traveling trader had been a help, at least. They had fairly definite information that Strong Bow had not perished on the Platte. The survivors specifically mentioned that he had not been with them on that fateful day.

Aiee, then where *was* he?

Some of South Wind's friends shook their heads and clucked their tongues over her reaction to the situation.

"She should realize that he is dead," said one sympathetically.

"Yes. She should do her mourning and be done with it . . . Let him go."

"But he is her baby," reminded another. "It is hardest to lose that one."

Eventually, one of them did make bold to suggest to South Wind that she face reality.

"Give him up, Wind," the woman suggested. "You cannot rest until you do. Come, I will mourn with you, for he was like a son to me, too, growing up with my own sons."

South Wind became furious, and ordered her friend from the lodge.

"He is *not* dead!" she shouted "It would be bad medicine to mourn someone who is not dead. It could even bring him harm."

So, people stopped mentioning her son, Strong Bow. Even her husband, White Fox, whose medicine was strong, had his doubts. Secretly, he cast the bones and was actually surprised when the patterns suggested that their son lived. However, the holy man did not speak of this to his wife. Sometimes the bones were wrong.

Now autumn was shortening the days, and Cold Maker's return was imminent. South Wind finished her preparations for the lodge, and was ready.

"I am made to think," she told her husband, "that Strong Bow will winter elsewhere. He will come back to us in the spring. Maybe for the Sun Dance."

"Maybe so," White Fox agreed.

But his heart was heavy. The two had been through much together, and had always talked of their troubles. This was something they seemed unable to share. It would be a long winter.

In the village on the Platte, Lone Elk watched the recovery of Bear Paws with great interest. He was pleased at the manner in which things had turned out. He had judged his man well, and he was pleased with himself.

Of course, there was no way he could have anticipated the enemy attack, or that it would prove the means for the acceptance of Bear Paws into the village. That had been pure good fortune. It was unfortunate about Laughing Crow, of course. His quick wit and good humor would be missed. The woman, too, though she had seemed to be becoming crazier anyway. But it was too bad.

There was something about that whole incident, though . . . the attack. When Lone Elk had picked up the robe that Bear Paws had dropped, a small packet had fallen out. It contained dried meat, enough for a few days. It had seemed insignificant at the time. In fact, he was not certain at first whether it had been carried by Bear Paws or by Laughing Crow. Crow had fallen quite close to the robe dropped by Bear Paws when he entered the fight. Why would *either* of them have carried supplies that morning?

That was something which had bothered Lone Elk for many days. It still did, to some extent. He could think of no reason for Crow to be planning a journey. Surely, he would have mentioned it to someone.

On the other hand, Bear Paws *might* have been leaving. The man seemed the type to be loyal to his own people, and to escape when he could. So probably, the packet of supplies had been carried by Bear Paws.

Another puzzle: No one had seemed to question what these four had been doing outside the village at dawn. Red Hand, Laughing Crow, Pumpkin Rings, and the prisoner. An odd assortment, except that they had this in common: Three of them wanted to kill the fourth. They had reason.

The only possible explanation that Lone Elk could decipher after the enemy was repulsed was this: Bear Paws had decided to escape, but had been discovered by the others, who were ready to stop him. Then the attack had come. Or did Bear Paws start to fight his way out *before* the attack? Probably not, he thought. The woman had been killed by a thrown ax, and Bear Paws had no ax. Crow was killed by an arrow. Bear Paws had shown skill with the bow, but in the fight he had used the bow of the fallen Crow. So if Crow was already dead, who had killed him? No, he died from an enemy arrow . . . Bear Paws was shooting Crow's own arrows.

But why was Red Hand's story of the fight so vague? And why, if Lone Elk's theory was correct, was Red Hand reluctant to tell of it? Puzzled, Lone Elk went back out to the site of the attack to reconnoiter. He had been a skilled tracker in his younger days. Maybe he could answer some of his questions.

He found the places where Crow and Pumpkin Rings had fallen. The grass and brush had been trampled somewhat, but he thought he could see where each had squatted or lain for a long time. All night, maybe . . . Red Hand? Elk did not know where he had stood, but his assailant's body had been there . . . shot from this angle . . . After some searching he found that spot, too. It was plainer, here, not so trampled, and easily seen as a place where someone had rolled in his robe for a night, or a large part of it.

So, the three *had* known. They had somehow discovered where, and on what night . . . The horse! Of course. The prized buffalo horse now claimed by Red Hand had been that of the prisoner. He would steal his own horse for his escape. Was this not where Red Hand liked to picket the animal to graze? Yes, it began to make sense now. The three had moved the horse and then hidden to wait for Bear Paws. This also would account for Red Hand's strange statement that Bear Paws had tried to warn them of the attack.

He walked around to where he believed Bear Paws would have been standing. Yes, the enemy had come across the slope, there, *behind* Crow and the woman. Bear Paws *had* probably warned them.

Now that he had decided what had happened, Lone Elk was undecided as to what he should do. He was still puzzled about Red Hand, and why the man was not telling the full facts of the case. The village had accepted Red Hand's account without question in the enormity of the total event. The story had been reinforced by an old man who had actually seen Bear Paws that morning. That one completely believed Red Hand's tale.

Well, Lone Elk decided, he would wait, watch, and see what happened.

It was several days later, when he was nearly asleep, that the answer came to him. He sat up, fully awake.

"What is it?" asked Kills-Three sleepily.

"It is nothing," he said, smiling in the darkness. But he had his answer.

There was no need to do or say anything. What was more, Red Hand had seen that immediately. As things were now, everyone was satisfied. The village had been saved by the captive, who was now a hero, and who showed increasingly a willingness to adapt to their ways. This was helped considerably, he was sure, by the romantic attentions of Pretty Sky.

This was what he had hoped for from the beginning. Lone Elk prided himself on his ability to judge a man. He had picked this one as a fighter. The enemy attack had certainly demonstrated that theory as a correct one.

From there it had gone well, too. It had been possible to play the three off against each other until the thirst for blood had quieted. Elk had perceived that there was actually a sort of friendship developing between the prisoner and Laughing Crow. An uneasy friendship for the captive, to be sure, but their joke, about whose hair Bear Paws was wearing . . . Ah, Laughing Crow would be missed.

And the increasing romance . . . That was good. He would be proud for his daughter to choose this proven warrior as her husband. It seemed to be going well. Each day Bear Paws seemed to be adapting better to their ways. It would not do to push him. Let him wear his hair in the fashion of his own people if he wished. It would take time. Kills-Three was working closely with Sky to see that the courtship moved at the proper speed. And what chance had a mere man against such a combination? He snuggled down in the robes next to Kills-Three and drifted off to sleep.

24
>> >> >>

Bear Paws recovered slowly from his wound, much more slowly than he anticipated. The musket ball had gone through cleanly, missing bone, but there was much damage to muscle. He could not effectively use the arm, though it was possible to move it a little. Of considerable annoyance was his inability to lift even the arm's own weight. As he sat, he could not even place the dangling hand in his lap without reaching to pick it up with the other.

His major concern, however, was weakness. Not weakness of the arm. He could understand that, and knew that the strength would return. He could even tell that the fingers of his left hand would still obey his wishes. He could move them properly. The weakness that made him want to cry out with frustration was a weakness of his whole body. He had lost a great quantity of blood, they told him.

When he was lying down, he noticed nothing amiss. But when he attempted to stand, or even sit up quickly, there was a sudden blackness that would descend on him for a moment. His ears would ring, and he would become so dizzy that he must lie back again, and try it more slowly.

He had plenty of help. Pretty Sky was always at his side, helping him, bringing him choice bits of food, or a gourd of cool water. Even Kills-Three seemed to have a complete change of attitude. Her harsh manner had completely mellowed now. She treated him like her own son. Possibly, even, she was more solicitous.

It was a radical change. At a time only three moons ago, he had been threatened, spat upon, beaten, and cruelly tied. The same people now almost revered him. He was a hero, a warrior who had stopped an enemy attack almost singlehanded. That interpretation was puzzling to him. He had had no lofty motives, no desire to be a hero to these people. Actually, he thought himself something of a coward. He had merely been forced to defend himself. He would not even have been in the place where the attack came if he had not been trying to run, to escape from his captivity.

There had apparently been only three who knew that. Pumpkin Rings and Laughing Crow were dead. Red Hand told a different story. Bear Paws had turned back the attack, killing two of the enemy singlehanded, saving the life of Red Hand, and rousing the sleeping village with his bloodcurdling battle cry.

Only one other person had seen the mighty Bear Paws that morning before the fight. He had risen from his bed to go outside the village and empty his bladder. There he had encountered Bear Paws, who was engaged in the same activity. They had exchanged greetings, the old man related. Bear Paws was acting strangely, but he had attributed that to the urgency of his errand. It was only later that he realized that Bear Paws was *already* suspicious, and had sensed something that was not right.

"He knew!" the old man said. "He went straight from there to see what was wrong. I was hardly back to bed when he gave the warning."

His wife supported the story.

"That is true! He was hardly back to bed!"

The old man's tale was quite logical, and helped to further the hero-image. Each time the story was repeated, it continued to grow.

What Bear Paws could not understand was the reaction of Red Hand. The clever warrior must have known . . . of course. The three who claimed rights to the prisoner had all been present. They had shared the knowledge of his escape attempt. Why, then, would Red Hand conceal this from the rest? It made no sense at all to Bear Paws, whose thinking was muddled anyway by the general weakness and lack of function brought on by blood loss.

He had had no chance to talk to Red Hand after the fight, and none presented itself for several days. It was a warm afternoon, and Bear Paws had not yet been out of the lodge. But he had been gaining strength, and could now walk across the room without becoming dizzy and light-headed.

"I will try to go outside," he signed to Pretty Sky.

"It is good," Kills-Three observed. "The sun is warm . . . You help him, Sky."

It was more difficult than he thought, this journey of a few steps. Even leaning on the strength of the girl, he was panting for breath and feeling faint when they stood in the open. His knees were wobbly and threatened to fold unexpectedly at any moment.

". . . sit . . ." he mumbled.

Though his words may not have been clear to Pretty Sky, the meaning certainly was.

"Here," she gestured. "On the lodge."

She helped him to lean, half-reclining, on the mound

that formed the dome of the earth-lodge, cradling his head on her shoulder. In a short while he felt much better. *Aiee*, it had been almost too much!

"You look better now," she told him. "You have more color in your face."

"But how will I get *back?*" he joked.

"Later. Rest a little. The sun will give you strength."

It was pleasant to rest in the sun, with the attentive Sky so concerned about his welfare. They lay there, watching clouds and a hawk high above, and listening to the soft murmur of the stream across the riffle. It was good.

This pleasant interlude was interrupted by the unexpected intrusion of Red Hand.

The warrior approached, and Bear Paws stiffened.

"What is it?" asked Pretty Sky in alarm.

"It is nothing," he told her, though he knew she would not believe him.

"Good day to you," Red Hand signed, smiling. "You are stronger, no?"

This friendly approach was somehow not very reassuring.

"Some better, yes," Bear Paws answered cautiously. "Still weak."

"That is to be. You lost much blood."

"So I am told."

There was a clumsy silence for a few moments.

"You are a brave man," Red Hand signed.

"No, no. I was only defending myself. I was much frightened."

"Who would not be? I was, too. What matters is what you *did.*"

Bear Paws was too tired and weak to argue.

"No," he insisted. "You know why I was there."

The eyes of Red Hand twinkled in amusement.

"Of course, Bear Paws. You heard or saw something that made you suspicious, no?"

Bear Paws was not certain of the motives of the other. Was Red Hand trying to reassure him that his secret was safe, or only toying with him, as a young fox plays with a mouse? He was too tired to decide.

"Maybe so," he signed. "I cannot remember."

Red Hand talked a little more of the weather and the warm day, and then sauntered off.

"What was that?" asked Pretty Sky.

"I do not know, Sky," he answered truthfully.

"He says you saved his life."

"Maybe. But he saved mine."

"It is good!" she said, giving him a quick hug.

Many times in later years, he was to puzzle over this strange reaction on the part of Red Hand. The man who had quite seriously claimed the right to kill him now seemed to regard the score as settled. It was as if his former enemy now considered that Bear Paws had redeemed himself. Perhaps, even, that the manner in which he had done so was rather amusing.

There was no question that Red Hand understood the failed escape attempt completely. Bear Paws' concern was whether the man would reveal what he knew. Very slowly, as the days passed, Bear Paws began to relax over that threat. With each passing day, the possibility seemed less threatening. Red Hand had held the power to destroy him, and had not done so. Whatever whim of grim humor had motivated this change, it was good.

For a long time, Bear Paws thought that he might discuss the subject again with Red Hand. Somehow, the appropriate time never came. First his weakness prevented moving about, then the two were seldom alone, and Bear Paws could think of no way to introduce the subject. Gradually, it began to seem less important, and the two never spoke of it again. There was no need.

Of course, Bear Paws' thoughts, as he grew stronger, turned again to leaving. He still felt the long-held urge to return to his own people. But now, the presence of Cold Maker was becoming more apparent. Mornings were frosty white. The leaves of the cottonwoods turned their spectacular golden yellow, fluttering in the golden sunlight of warm afternoons. The oaks and maples, though scarce here, brightened the landscape with their splashes of crimson. Then all too soon, the colors of autumn were gone. Almost overnight, it seemed, the trees performed their ritual, and the Moon of Falling Leaves was gone.

Winter was coming. Squirrels frantically gathered nuts and planted or stored them. It was the rutting season of the deer, and the bucks fought for possession of the females. Every day, the bugling of young bull elk could be heard in the distance. Their behavior was unpredictable, somewhat dangerous. Quail, too, were unpredictable, flying wildly in unlikely directions. Migrating birds behaved strangely.

There was little hunting, because the fall buffalo hunt had been quite successful, and their meat was of better quality anyway than that of deer or elk. Days were growing shorter, which added to the general unrest. It was the Moon of Madness.

This restlessness also pervaded the recovery of Bear Paws. He was growing rapidly stronger now, which made him all the more impatient with the frustration that he now faced. It took him a while to admit to himself that the season was becoming too late for him to travel. By the time he regained enough strength for such a journey, the weather would be too unpredictable. He could not risk the possibility of being caught without shelter in a sudden early snow. Even so, he was quite reluctant to admit to the obvious conclusion: He must spend the winter here, with the Pawnees.

He spent much time in thought. The People would be moving into winter camp now. His own Southern band would probably be wintering at the far southern edge of their range. The scrub oak thickets in that region were excellent protection from Cold Maker's icy blasts. Their dead leaves clung to the branches all winter, an effective windbreak for a skin lodge.

His mother would be cutting the thick clumps of frost-dried tallgrass to stuff into the storage space around the base of the lodge for warmth. He wondered whether the great fall hunt of the People had gone well. He regretted now the manner in which he and his family had parted. His indignant defiance now seemed a trifle childish, and he was embarrassed when he thought of it. It had nearly caused his death on two occasions now. He wondered if they thought him dead. He was sorry to have caused them concern, but there was little he could do now. There was no way even to send them word that he was alive. That would have to wait.

And waiting was extremely frustrating for an active young man. He tried to fit into the activities of his former captors, who now accepted him as one of their own. This was only moderately successful.

His mixed feelings were confused even further by the presence of the girl, Pretty Sky. He had always thought her one of the most beautiful of women. She had probably saved his life. She had made it her primary activity to look after his needs and nurse him back to health. It was extremely pleasant to be with her. It made him forget for a while, forget to wonder what his own people were doing, where they might be camped for the winter, how the fall hunt had been. Her presence, in fact, made him forget everything else, everything but her presence.

He began to think in terms of how *she* would react to various events, sights, or sounds. The call of a hunting owl, a doe with twin fawns. On a walk one morning, alone, he saw a fox pup running in circles, apparently for the pure joy of running. *I must tell Sky about it,* he thought, wishing that she could have seen, too.

Very subtly, in many ways, he was beginning to miss her at any time they were not together. Still, it was well into the Moon of Long Nights before he realized what was happening to him. Then realization struck him forcibly, and in the form of a question.

Would it be possible, when spring came, for him to leave these people and return to his own? Close on the heels of that question came another: Why would he even *want* to?

Epilogue

›› ›› ››

Governor Valverde sat at his desk and stared at the wall in despair. His world was falling apart around him. The situation had seemed more threatening with each interview, each pitiful survivor that came to tell his story.

I should have gone myself, Valverde thought. But then, of course, *his* bones might lie moldering on the Platte, instead of those of the hapless Villasur.

The ironic twist was that Villasur seemed to have handled the expedition well. The descriptions furnished by the tattered remnants of the command would indicate that. As a commander in the field, the Lieutenant Governor had appeared decisively in control. Except, of course, that he had been no match for the European-trained French commanders of the savages.

"But, Excellency, we saw no French!" one of the first interviewees had protested.

Valverde's fist crashed down on his desk so hard that the inkwell bounced, rocking the dark fluid that half filled it. An orderly glanced in through the doorway, sized up the anger in his commander's face in an instant, and retreated.

"Of course there were French!" the Governor hissed. "You said there were volleys of musket fire!"

"Muskets, yes, sir," the terrified sergeant mumbled. "But . . . volleys?"

"And where would they get muskets?" Valverde persisted, ignoring the obvious military distinction between ordered volleys and sporadic fire. "From *us?*"

"No, sir."

"Then there must have been French!"

"Yes, sir." The sergeant had not earned his stripes by contradicting the opinions of his superiors.

"Well, then . . . how many?"

"Ah . . . I saw no more than three, Excellency."

Word passed quickly, and later survivors who were interviewed in the Governor's office had seen at least a dozen French troops in tricorn hats and pantaloons fighting among the savage attackers.

This made the Governor feel somewhat more justified, although not much. The responsibility for the defeat was still his. The letter from the Viceroy had been quite specific. He, Valverde, had been expected to lead that expedition. And he, Valverde, must be the one to report the outcome. If there were only some way to distract attention . . . Make a martyr, perhaps, out of Villasur. It was true that Villasur's command had been attacked while technically under a flag of truce. Ah, yes . . . *treachery!* If he could rouse the ire of the high command at the treachery of the enemy, maybe his own actions, or lack thereof, would be overlooked. It was worth a try.

He reached for one of the quills in the penholder, and examined its tip. Carefully, he pared the point, dipped in the inkwell, and tested a few strokes on a scrap of parchment. Then he drew forth a new sheet and began to write.

To His Excellency, Viceroy of Mexico, greetings and salutations.

It is my painful duty to report on our military expedition to the plains, as per Your Excellency's request.

After a false start or two, and much thought, the Governor began to warm to his task. He described Villasur's diplomatic successes with the towns he encountered, and the final defeat through treachery on the part of the French.

He was interrupted by a knock at his door. One of the priests, who held a skin in his hands . . .

"Excellency, one of our mission natives has sketched a scene . . . He was with the Lieutenant Governor at the battle. This man shows great talent."

"Not now, padre," Valverde waved him away. "I am busy with a communication."

The disappointed priest was nearly through the outer office before an idea struck the Governor. Had not the chaplain been killed?

"Wait," he called. "Come back, padre."

The crude paintings were actually quite good, in a primitive, savage way. Yes . . . quite acceptable for his purpose. Rapidly, he outlined his ideas.

". . . a painting, on hides, padre! Big! As big as this wall. It must show the heroic deaths of our beloved Pedro de Villasur and his men. French soldiers here, perhaps. The junction of the rivers . . ."

As the delighted padre left the room, Valverde turned back to his desk, pleased with himself. He would inform the Viceroy that a commemorative painting had been commissioned, in honor of the noble dead. It would show the treachery, and the Viceroy would understand that the military situation had been little short of hopeless from the first, against such an enemy.

He picked up his pen, wiped the quill, and redipped it.

"The heretical Huguenots," he wrote, *"did not even spare the innocence of the priest."*

GENEALOGY

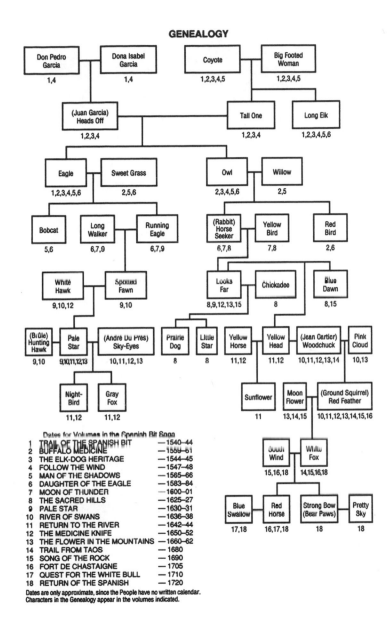

Dates for Volumes in the Spanish Bit Saga

1	TRAIL OF THE SPANISH BIT	—1540–44
2	BUFFALO MEDICINE	—1559–61
3	THE ELK-DOG HERITAGE	—1544–45
4	FOLLOW THE WIND	—1547–48
5	MAN OF THE SHADOWS	—1565–66
6	DAUGHTER OF THE EAGLE	—1583–84
7	MOON OF THUNDER	—1600–01
8	THE SACRED HILLS	—1625–27
9	PALE STAR	—1630–31
10	RIVER OF SWANS	—1636–38
11	RETURN TO THE RIVER	—1642–44
12	THE MEDICINE KNIFE	—1650–52
13	THE FLOWER IN THE MOUNTAINS	—1660–62
14	TRAIL FROM TAOS	—1680
15	SONG OF THE ROCK	—1690
16	FORT DE CHASTAIGNE	—1705
17	QUEST FOR THE WHITE BULL	—1710
18	RETURN OF THE SPANISH	—1720

Dates are only approximate, since the People have no written calendar.
Characters in the Genealogy appear in the volumes indicated.

Don Coldsmith was born in Iola, Kansas, in 1926. He served as a World War II combat medic in the South Pacific and returned to his native state, where he graduated from Baker University in 1949 and received his M.D. from the University of Kansas in 1958. He worked at several jobs before entering medical school: He was a YMCA Youth Director, a gunsmith, a taxidermist, and for a short time a Congregational preacher. In addition to his private medical practice, Dr. Coldsmith has been a staff physician at Emporia State University's Health Center, where he also teaches in the English Department. He discontinued medical pursuits in 1990 to devote more time to his writing. He and his wife Edna, of thirty years, operate a small cattle ranch. They have raised five daughters.

Dr. Coldsmith produced the first ten novels in the Spanish Bit Saga in a five-year period; he writes and revises the stories first in his head, then in longhand. From this manuscript the finished version is skillfully typed by his longtime secretary.

Of his decision to create, or re-create, the world of the Plains Indian in the early centuries of European contact, the author says: "There has been very little written about this time period. I wanted also to portray these Native Americans as human beings, rather than as stereotyped 'Indians.' That word does not appear anywhere in the series, for a reason. As I have researched the time and place, the indigenous cultures, it's been a truly inspiring experience for me."